T0193125

Blair
and the
Blue
Rose

Nero Aries

authorHOUSE®

AuthorHouse™
1663 Liberty Drive
Bloomington, IN 47403
www.authorhouse.com
Phone: 1 (800) 839-8640

Published by AuthorHouse 03/15/2019

ISBN: 978-1-7283-0454-0 (sc)
ISBN: 978-1-7283-0453-3 (e)

CHAPTER 1

What a Peculiar Thing

I remember the smell of home; it always smelled like rain. The little three bedroom house with the gray panel siding that my family and I lived in, on the corner of Thirteenth and Charnel Street. I never thought I'd get tired of Seattle, until my parents decided we should go on that stupid family trip to visit my aunt Velma and her drunkard husband in Canada. I remember the transition of scenery from the shimmering, rain covered streets to the world turning white with snow. My little sister, Emma, was so annoying the whole trip; I bet she asked me a thousand questions. I remember my parents playing their mixtapes of Elvis, Frank Sinatra, and a few others I didn't know, the whole way up there. It was my Seventeenth birthday. My dad was so proud of the handcrafted silver cross necklace with the blue sapphire in the center that he had bought me. I was never big on jewelry, but I really liked it. Funny to think it's only been six months. I remember my mom turning up the heater when I was cold and didn't want to say anything, and my boyfriend, Damien, wrapping his arms around me. Mom's cherry red lipstick.. and such a pretty smile. She surprised me with two tickets to see my favorite band back in December; I still have them in the coffin shaped birthday card they picked out. I remember the smell of dad's coffee, and of mom's perfume. And I remember those god awful sounds.. the tires squealing, and the front of the car crushing as it met the tree. The mortifying sight of seeing that limb burst through the windshield, impaling my father and his headrest, and hearing my little sister's neck snap against the back of the seat. I remember watching my mother being ejected head first through the shards of shattering glass, and her lifeless body sliding across the frozen ground. I ran to help her, only to turn and see the car going up in flames, and Damien struggling to get out of his stuck seatbelt.. his soft lips motioning "I love you" as he choked on his last breath.

I remember it all....

Happy fucking birthday, Blair.

After the tragedy, I ended up staying with my aunt Velma. I had no other family, and no money to make it on my own. It was a lot different than it was back home, but it wasn't not too bad, I guess. I'd become rather fond of the silence and solitude, and my aunt and uncle are mostly quiet. Velma sits by the fire in her rocker and reads romance novels most days, and her husband, uncle Cid, is either passing out in the barn, drunk, or hunting in the nearby woods. I don't like the vibes or weird looks I get from him. The alone time lets me reflect. The most communication I get is from my therapist, whom seems to care about my thoughts and feelings about as much as a maggot cares whose corpse it's eating. There isn't even a phone here for me to call my old friends. So, to say the least, I am utterly and completely alone now.

The aesthetics of this place are still settling in for me, as well. The suburban lifestyle I've known for so long has been replaced with a stone cottage that is literally in the middle of nowhere. The cottage consists of the kitchen, living room, a restroom, one upstairs bedroom, and a closet under the staircase; they were kind enough to let me sleep in the closet. There is the rundown barn that uncle Cid uses to store the old Chevy truck he'll never restore, and is where he keeps all his booze (which I occasionally sneak into to fill my skull shaped flask.) Other than that, there is a poorly made carport for their station wagon, a small shed, and a large garden. Though I've never seen anyone tend to it, the garden's large hedges and pink roses seem to be growing quite luscious. This is the place I find myself spending most of my time. It's a big garden, but feels like a labyrinth as I wonder aimlessly. It's nice to just be able to escape from this drab space. Hours will pass, and by the time I realize how long I've been out, my entire body feels dead... numb.. from the cold atmosphere. Yet, still, this is my only place of happiness in such a sorrowful world. I still can't figure out why my parents wanted to visit here in the first place.

Anyways, the garden is where our story really begins. Walls of green with accents of pink surround me, the soft white snow crunching beneath my feet, birds singing like some sort of old Disney movie, and the pale blue sky just sitting gracefully above; I didn't even know songbirds could survive in this climate, but it was nice. Speaking of the climate, I really should've packed better clothes, but aunt Velma lets me borrow her fur coat when I come out. Still, these black suede slippers aren't made to ice hike. As I strolled, I seemed to continuously find paths I hadn't walked, as there were no footprints. Walking along, the birds' song began to become more and more quiet. Silenced completely, I found myself before a small tree with a trunk merely ten or so feet tall, dark leaves, and black foliage climbing the bark and covering the ground around it. The thing that stood out the most was the rose emitting from the mondo grass. Whilst the rest of the garden was filled with these dull, pink roses, this rose was blue and almost seemed to glow. The beauty in what I'd discovered was nearly enough to take my breath away. Its petals were soft as a baby's touch, and the smell was alluring and mysterious. As I admired its presence, I could hear aunt Velma calling me for dinner. I picked the rose and followed my footsteps back to the cottage. Probably should've left it there.

Plain oatmeal for dinner and a glass of flavorless sparkling water. Cid ate a large bowl with a tankard of ale, and Velma didn't eat; I don't think she ever eats. Dinner conversation was a perfect match to the rest of the events here: lonely and silent. After dinner, I went to my room to write about my day. I didn't finish all of the water, so that I could keep the blue rose in my glass like a vase. This room is bullshit.. just a daybed and a small dresser crammed in a four by six room with Christmas lights that I nailed around the ceiling. Aunt Velma is still pissed about the anarchy symbol I drew on the wall with my nail polish. At least it gave the room a little character.

Hours passed, and after writing I needed to find something to do. There's no tv here, and I really don't feel like drawing right now. I reached under the red knit mattress for my flask.. empty. Guess it's time to re-up. I put on the fur coat over my Nightmare Before Christmas pajamas and grabbed my dad's old flashlight, then slowly opened the door. No sign of anyone being awake. I took a quick peak into their bedroom and saw that they were both asleep. It's so weird that they sleep in separate beds. I slipped out back and made my way towards the barn. It felt as if I were being watched. Artic wolves are native to this area, but I'm almost there. Once inside the barn, I turned on the flashlight and went into the back room. Jackpot! I found an unopened bottle of Pumpkin Spice Rum.. my favorite. The bottle was old and dusty, so it's probably been here for a while, and it will likely go unnoticed if I just take the whole-

BANG

A loud noise came from the other room.. followed by very light footsteps. I turned the light off and hid behind an old saddle rack. The door of the storage room slowly creaked open a little, and I could hear a growl under hungry breath. The door opened, and moonlight gleamed in.. revealing the large, white wolf sniffing me out. He kept his nose to the floor, coming closer. His big head knocked over liquor bottles as he searched the lower shelves where I was. Closer. There is nowhere else for him to look now but where I am. Closer. He begins to growl as he comes within the meter. Closer. Snarling and barking, our eyes interlock. The great beast lunges and-

POW!

My ears were ringing in pain and the room filled with gun smoke.

"Blair?", called uncle Cid, shining his light at me, "The hell you doing out here in the middle of the night?"

I stood up and stepped out, hiding the bottle under my arm, "I just.. I just needed some fresh air, I-" he interrupted me, sliding his hand in my coat and grabbing the bottle.

I could smell the heavy alcohol on his breath.

He looked down at the bottle and chuckled, "You weren't planning on taking this, were you? Pretty young girls shouldn't be out here all alone.. vulnerable. There's bad stuff out here. Could get hurt," he came closer, forcing me against the counter and pressing the hot barrel of his rifle into my private areas, "Could get really hurt," his filthy hand began to slide under my shirt, "Might even get- *OOF!!*"

I slammed my knee into the sick bastard's groin and

knocked him in the head with the rum bottle; He fell to the ground unconscious. Tears filling my eyes, I ran back to the cottage as fast as I could and locked myself in my room. I couldn't help but think of Damien, and how I've kept my virginity for him all these years, ever since we'd met in grade school; we were saving ourselves for marriage. When I got back to the house, I was shaking with fear, and ended up drinking the entire bottle that night. I also resorted to the only sort of release I've ever known.. splitting my wrist to try and bleed out the pain. I don't know if it was the alcohol, anxiety, or blood loss, but I eventually passed out. I was plagued by strange dreams of being tortured by ancient devices in a small caged room with the word 'Fenrir' scraped over the chained doorframe.

I woke up the next morning, eyes still wet and my bloody wrist dried to the white pillowcase. At this point, my entire existence has become nothing more than a spiraling array of discombobulation and melancholy, however, the rose in the cup of water managed to hone my attention. The brilliant blue rose had wilted overnight, and somehow changed to the plain pink pigment of those others in the garden. How peculiar. For several days, I only left my room to get food and use the restroom. Other than that, I kept the door locked and just tried to sleep. No one ever even came to check on me. It was a Sunday morning when I decided to come out. I missed the garden, so I unlocked the door and began my day. Neither Velma nor Cid were anywhere to be found. I sat in the living room for awhile before going out to the shed... this is where all of Damien's and my parents' stuff was put. The lock was a bit frozen, but Cid kept his tools here and I found an ice pick to chiseled off what I needed to, afterwards tucking the pick into my belt. I began riffling and the memories began rolling. And with the memories came more tears. I really miss them. I took a few old pictures that dad had in his wallet, Damien's black knitted blanket, Emma's stuffed rabbit, and the Polaroid camera that my mom used to use for her photography business. I think I'll take some pictures of the garden.

Ff nN Ir r

eE Rr R

There was still no one home, and I'm happy about that. I started going through my clothes and decided to wear my favorite outfit. I put on my low cut black corset dress with the white skulls, fishnet stockings and gloves, my black platform boots, and a big black bow in my hair. Oh, and my nails are, of course, black, and I have the black/purple dead look going on with my eye shadow, and my mom's red lipstick. I am ready now. I went out to the garden and casually walked around. It always feels better here when I'm lost. The birds were less chatty, but I managed to get a few pictures of them. Other than that, it was mostly scenery. I daydreamed as I walked. I thought of home, and of going back. I could always just take their car.. but I'd probably get arrested at border patrol or something. Still, I'd probably be living better off in jail than I am now. I thought of how much I hated school, but also how much I missed it. All my friends, the lunches that actually weren't that bad, and my crazy choir teacher that always wore way too much make-up. I thought of everything.. and everyone... that I took for granted. But honestly... there wasn't really anything left to go back to now.

As I pondered on life, I saw a little black bunny flash across the snow. I want to take a picture of him! I started to chase him this way and that way, aimlessly, taking random trails, trying to catch up. "Excuse me, wait up!!" I yelled. And just as I was running out of breath, he disappeared into the black foliage. Under that small tree. And you wouldn't believe what was there..... It was that same blue rose, growing in that same exact spot. But how.. how is that even possible? There was only one when I picked it, and it is simply impossible for it to have grown back already, yet.. here it is. Its right-

"Well, well.. we meet again" said a deep voice from behind me. I turned around, and there he was. It was Cid, holding that same rifle. "It wasn't very nice hitting me like that the other night. Matter of fact, it was downright rude."

There was evil in his hick voice, and I felt my heart sink further with each step closer he took.

"Now, we're gonna finish what we started the other night," he said while unfastening his belt, "and you'd better just be a good girl and take it, or there might be an accident... Velma knows these bullets tend to ricochet."

He got in my face and stroked my hair.

"Bend over, bitch." he whispered angrily.

"Please, no.. just stop.." but he just laughed and started getting rough, then he pushed me into the black grass and slid his pants down.

I could feel the thorns from the blue rose stabbing my back. I struggled and fought as he pulled up my dress and tried to force himself inside of me.

The sick fuck had nearly penetrated my sanctuary, but suddenly I remembered something vital and screamed, "I said stop it you fucking psycho!!"

Grabbing the ice pick from my belt, plunging it into his throat. He stumbled backwards and stood up. I arose, as well, in a dire panic.

"You stup- *gurgle, gurgle* stupid *cough* stupid little bitch!"

Blood gushing from his jugular, Cid raised his gun with the strength he had left and squeezed the trigger, with me in his sights. I remember hearing silence, rather than a gunshot. I remember that warm pressure of the bullet on my chest amongst the chilling air. I remember the blood gushing from his neck as he fell dead from pulling out the ice pick, and that white wolf standing behind him with crimson dripping from his jaws. I remember the ground feeling like water as I sank into it through the black grass. And I remember that brilliant blue rose glowing in my hands as the world fell to shadows.

CHAPTER 2

Reality is but a Far Off Dream

It's a funny thing, really; the things we do based on natural instinct. Wolves run on their toes for increased speed and dexterity, to aid them in the hunt for prey. A shark doesn't have to be told to keep moving in the ocean if it wants to continue breathing. The basic instincts of survival are programmed into the DNA of each species. Why? Because, in the end, all any of us want to do is survive. As for me, I don't even know where I am anymore. Everything feels like a deep hallucination. I don't even feel real. What am I? Am I still breathing? Am I still.. alive? I'm just... floating.. through this black empty space. Falling in slow motion. I remember..... Actually, I don't remember much of anything right now. I feel so tired. So fuzzy.. 'Fenrir?' odd voices reverberated in my head. Who's Fenrir? What a silly name. Can you help me? Hello? Where did you go? Please, help me! Someone? Anyone? Mom.? Dad...? .....anyone?

Minutes pass, and the silence was finally broken by a deep, dark voice, "Blair. Blair Sterling. You are dead. Deceased by a lead projectile piercing and obliterating your cardiovascular system. You-"

"Excuse me, sir. Who are you? Please, I need help", I interrupted.

The irritated voice of power replied, "Female mortal, have you not heard my words? You are dead, and I am Sir Death, here to walk you through the afterlife. Now, f-"

"The.. the afterlife? So I am dead, then.. Please, Mr.

Death, are you going to take me to see my loved ones? I'd like to see my parents. They passed away a few months ago, and."

More irritated than before, "Firstly, it's SIR DEATH. Mr. Death was my father. Secondly, you cannot get to Heaven, and neither are those in recent loss there. Now, I will guide you through purgatory and-"

"Can't go to Heaven? And just why the hell not? What have I done that's so wrong? And my parents were great people. I know damn well they-"

Sir Death interrupts me this time, "Slow down, slow down! It's not that simple, my dear. Here, allow me to explain: Normally, when a person dies, they come here, to purgatory. It is in this place that I have knowledge of that person's life and may decide their fate. If the spirit is a good one, we rise to Heaven. If they are bad, I cast them into Hell! But.. there has been a complication. When a person's fate cannot be so easily decided, or when they cannot be read so easily, or try to cheat me, they are sent to Deadland; the space in between the space in between spaces. God rules Heaven, Satan rules Hell, I rule purgatory, and the Velvet Queen rules Deadland. Over the years, the Velvet Queen has become envious of the other realms, as they receive a multitude more of souls than she, and seeks now to steal the dead. All of them. She has managed to block the passages to Heaven and Hell. Souls cannot survive here, and therefore have no choice but to pass on to her world. With these passages closed, souls are being lost in the wasteland. I am sorry, but though this is where your parents are, you will likely never see them again, even in death. Now, come. Your soul won't last much longer here. We must-"

"But, Sir Death! There must be a way to reopen Heaven."

Sir Death paused, contemplating, and in a grave voice replies, "That, my dear, is beyond you."

It was at that moment in time that the calm darkness surrounding me began to spin in chaos and swirl with ominous hues of green until I became completely unconscious from the nausea.

My dreary eyes opened and the world around me was an obstructed daze; like dropping acid and watching My Little Pony. As the scenery gained structure, I found myself lying in a lush black forest under a crackling red sky. It's been awhile since I felt such warm weather. Everything was so odd, and mysteriously delightful. What now, though? I'm in a place I know nothing about, and Sir Death said I'd not find my parents.

"Oh, I just don't know what to do!" I fitted aloud. The confusion and delusion worsened the more I thought about my situation. Did I really just have a conversation with someone claiming to be Death.?

I heard several voices amongst the trees go back and forth, "A new arrival," "What a weird girl," "Get that girl a chaperone?" "She's clearly lost." Where are these voices coming from? I don't see any one. "H-Hello? Is someone there?" I asked. "Yes, over here, woman." Still, I see no one.

"Where arc you? Come out this instant." I replied to the voice.

"Come out? Why, I'm always out!"

And then I saw him. The face on the tree.. and it's talking to me!

"Why, you're a talking tree!"

The smug tree mocked me, "Why, you're a talking buildup of calcium covered in flesh!" Clearly I had upset him.

"I'm sorry. I'm just not used to the trees speaking to me where I'm from. I'm Blair; pleased to meet you, sir."

He looked at me with a relaxed face, "The trees are always talking, no matter where you're from. It's only a matter of whether or not you are willing to listen. You may call me Mr. Elmsworth. Now, what has you in such distress?"

I looked down, and said to the arbor gentleman, "I am so terribly lost and have no idea what to do. I don't know where I am exactly or where I should go, or even what I am exactly."

"Well, you are a new arrival, you should probably start by finding a place to stay. This is a very dangerous place. Just steer of the Velvet Bitch.. erumm... I mean, Velvet Queen. She is the ruler of this realm, and she is as nasty as she is lovely. We trees are happy here in the open forest, but it is no place for a flesh-bag such as yourself.. you'd be gobbled up. Ah, and as for who you are. We all have a purpose, and as with all things, it will reveal itself at correct moment in time, so don't worry about that. Life and death can be so context sensitive. Haha! But, you have nowhere to go and nothing to do, so not knowing where you are is right where you need to be. Right?"

His words were interrupted by loud footsteps that shook the treetops.

The tree's voice trembled, "Oh dear.. that doesn't sound good. Blair, sorry to cut our conversation so short, but quickly, you must hide. In here!" A nearby tree trunk opened to be hollow, and I was swooped inside by an array of tentacle like vines. "Be VERY quiet!" he whispered.

Moments later, a... man-like creature with the body and horns of a bull, with red fur and bone armor, standing a brooding thirty feet high or taller, approached the talking trees.

He drew his giant double sided scythe, and, with a demanding voice, stated, "I am here upon the official order of the Velvet Queen. Two spirits have escaped from the castle's Soul Chamber, and have therefore committed treason against Deadland and her people. In addition, multiple new arrivals have been sensed and have not yet given their legally required oaths to servitude and slavery, as is by law under the Red Order. If you have any information, speak now, otherwise, if you are found knowledgeable, you will also be charged with treason and punished with death."

The trees mostly remained quiet, save for a few whispers amongst themselves.

The large man beast, angered from being ignored, swung his scythe and cut through four trees with ease, "I'm only asking nicely one more time before I turn your entire happy little forest into a petrified ruin. Where's the girl? I know she dropped here.. and she–" Mr. Elmsworth snapped back, "She's already gone! Left an hour ago.. due south, towards the marsh. Now, leave us be; we have a truce."

The beast smirked and got in his face, "See, now that wasn't so hard. Next time, you'd all do good to answer a royal official the first time he asks a question. Let this serve as a reminder."

He placed his hoof on Mr. Elmsworth and mumbled something under his breath, then began to walk away, "Fuck your truce. All hail the Velvet Queen!" he shouted and galloped away. The hoof mark remained on the tree and began to petrify

"Blair," the tree spoke to me, "I don't know what it is, but you are special. I can sense a hero in you, and the Velvet Queen herself has already sent her Deathborn after you. I want you to go north. It's a full day's walk from here, but look for a giant stone sword penetrating the top of a flat mountain. This is known as Hero's Respite, and it is the place where the champions of the worlds go to pray for guidance. I do not know where your path will take you, but you will do great things."

The hoof mark had spread infectiously to petrify the entire tree. As the stone encased completely, Mr. Elmsworth crumbled into thousands of small rock particles, and from the rubble arose the spirit of the tree in the form of a light pink, luminescent butterfly. It flew around me a few times, then landed on my chest... Hm, how troubled of me not to have noticed it before, but a tattoo of a blue rose has somehow scarred itself around my collar bone. It's so soft to the touch that it feels like real petals. The butterfly landed on it, just before fading away.

"Alright," I said aloud in a teary voice, "North." ..before that thing shows back up.

I started my journey, and the forest seemed to be never-ending. I saw a lot of familiar creatures, with not so familiar features. The birds, for instance, are not singing joyful songs, but carry a rather grimace tone and have eyes that glow like stars. Tentacles lurking in the streams, sharks with wings, such peculiar things indeed. By nightfall, I found myself still surrounded by trees. The pale green moon arose brightly, shaped like a skull. I tried asking the trees for shelter, yet they have become far less willing to communicate.. due to the incident, I'm sure. Monsters walked in the dark. Rotting corpses dragging their limbs, moaning and growling. The zombies moved in hordes, but seemed not to notice me. I moved away quietly until they were completely out of sight and I could no longer hear them. There in the night, beneath a thorny black bush, I laid my head on fallen leaves with the hope that I may rest, but the wolven howls in the distance are such a fright. The skull moon was also eerie; its eyes seemed to glare intimidatingly into mine. An hour or so passed with me lying here, and my tummy began to rumble fiercely. I'm so hungry. I did, however, eventually fall to slumber. Finally.

Morning light beamed over me, and I was awoken by a familiar sound.

"Blair?", it called, "Blair, wake up! Blair!"

I open my eyes to the noise. The sunlight is pretty bright, but I can make out a blurry figure standing above me.

"Blair, sweetie!" Is that... could it be.? "M-mom.? Mom, is... you're here?!"

I jumped up quickly and hugged her so tightly, "Mom! Oh my God! Mom, I'm so happy to see you!"

Tears of joy poured from my eyes, "I thought I'd never find you! Sir Death said-"

"Sir Death is a fool," she snapped, before reverting to her alluring tone, "I mean, I'm here, sweetie."

She hugged me tighter. The world was much less chaotic in the daytime. The trees, the grass, the sun. It all looked so normal.

"Oh, how I've missed you, too, sweetheart. Come now, your father will be so thrilled to see you."

We walked a ways down a nearby trail until arriving at a small community. By the time we got there, it had begun to rain. I've missed the rain. We went into the house where my dad was cooking breakfast; bacon and swiss omelets.. my favorite. We sat at the table together and ate as a family. I found it odd that we didn't say grace, but I guess there isn't much of a point of praying once you get to a place like this. I told them of my horrible experience staying with aunt Velma and uncle Cid, and of the rose and wolf and all that happened since I was shot. I never thought exchanging death stories would be considered acceptable breakfast conversation, alas, I don't think much would surprise me at this point. I asked about Damien and Emma, but they hadn't found them yet. The house was simple, but it was comfortable and felt like a home.

"Hey, kiddo.. check this out," my dad said as he grabbed my hand.

He took me down the hall and motioned me to open the door. It looked almost identical to my room back in Seattle. They even took the time to paint some of my old posters on the walls. Mom and dad always did go the extra mile to make sure I was happy. Tears filled my eyes as I hugged my dad in silence. We spent the day talking and walking the nearby area; dad even killed a deer with his bow. Later that night, said deer was butchered and served for dinner. We had charred venison, steamed peppers, fresh sliced bread, and red wine. Deadland may seem like a pretty messed up place, but being back with my family so soon.. it was proving to have its perks. I took a nice, long, hot shower, then they tucked me into bed, kissed my forehead, and turned out the light. The moon was full, and its gentle light swayed in my room. It also began to storm a bit harder. I remember lying in bed when I was a little girl, and getting up to play in the middle of the night. I'd dance with my dolls in the moonlight. As another hour or so passed, the storm worsened and I became slightly hungry again, and I remember seeing a red velvet cake in the kitchen.

I made my way out and cut a slice, then sat down at the table to eat. The soft red had such a smooth chocolaty flavor, and the lemon hinted cream cheese frosting was divine.

I finished my last bite, and heard my dad's voice from behind me, "Sweetheart, what are you doing up? Everything okay?"

I answered with a smile, "Yeah, dad. Just grabbing a bite."

It was quiet for a few moments before he said anything, "Sssuch a ssssweet girl. Daddy wantss a bite..."

The hiss in his voice.

I felt my heart sink, "D-dad.?"

I turned around, trembling, to find the face and voice on my father on a humanoid snake-like creature with thick green venom creeping from his long fangs, and one of the same ilk, with characteristics of my mother, soon entered the room, as well.

"What the hell is this?!" I screamed.

"You shhhouldn't ssspeak to your parentsss that way. Now ssstay sstill!"

They slithered towards me in a winding motion, striking and hissing, becoming angrier as they tried to eat me. I ran to my room in panic and locked the door behind me. What the hell is going on? What's wrong with my parents? They pound at the door, hissing and threatening me. I scrounged around for a proper place to hide or for something I could use as a weapon, but there is nothing. Seconds later, chunks of wood blew across the room as they smashed the door in. What do I do? What do I do?? The window! I dived head first through the glass just before they could impale me with those poisonous jaws, but this had no delay on the pursuit. I was cut pretty badly. They were still right behind me, closing in. I ran through the village and more of the serpentine joined the chase. The forest echoed with rattles and hissing, and all I could do is hide. I used the darkness to my advantage and slipped away long enough to climb a tree and hope it was good enough. I could make out their shapes slithering on the dark woodland floor below. All I have to do is remain quiet and,

"*Aggk!!!*" I screamed out loud at the sharp pain in my leg.

There were no snakes in the tree with me, but I could feel the blood pouring from my leg. The scream attracted the snakes. As they swarmed, the moonlight intensified with a bright red illumination and bits of the sky fell. As they began wrapping around me, the red light became so powerful that it blinded me completely and eliminated all sound. And then I woke up. Still curled up under that black bush. Red sunlight beaming through the clouds, and a light rain that looked like blood drops. It was.. it was all just a dream? But.. my parents. They were *ouch!* I gasped in pain! My leg was hurt and I could feel a tight pressure at my calf. I pulled my leg up and brushed off the leaves to reveal my wound. And it was a bite mark... The bite mark of a wolf.

CHAPTER 3

A Bad Girl and One Good Boy

The bloody rain was a light drizzle, and the sun was hidden by the dreary, low hanging, iron gray clouds. I stood to my feet and continued my journey towards Hero's Respite, no matter how pointless it actually seemed to me. The bleeding of my leg had mostly ceased, but the swelling and pain still made it difficult to walk. I passed many trees with faces, and they spoke not a single word. I finally broke the tree line, and found myself standing now before an enormous open field. The grass was tall, about knee high, and there was just a single tree growing in the center. My eyes grew wide as I realized what magnificent beauty I had stumbled upon. My mouth began to salivate like a slit throat and my tummy gave a rumble that shook the Heavens.. it's a fucking apple tree!! I darted towards it, ready to eat each and every plump fruit hanging from its limbs. However, the further I ran, the more difficult it became to move. The grass seems to be getting higher and higher the closer I get, and the green blades slit my skin like paper-cuts. And it's honestly irrelevant. My hunger at this point is enough to allow me to ignore the pain and keep moving. Breast high is the grass. Must keep going. Shoulder high. Must.. ugh, fuck.. it kinda stings now. Once the grass reached above my head, it quickly began to tower hundreds of feet high, and even the width seemed of colossal proportion. The benefit of this, though, is being able to walk around the blades, rather that it cut me. I walked a bit more, and felt as if I were not alone. The pitter patter of small footsteps trotted lightly around me, hiding behind the giant plants and large rocks.

"Who's there? Come out! Come out now!"

And just as I finished, I saw the cutest things; three little vintner colored flying squirrels popped to my attention. And these aren't the flying squirrels I remember. Rather than webbing, they had beautiful, fluffy wings. They began to chatter happily and dance around me.

"Excuse me," I asked, "do you know how to get to the tree?" Looking at me confused, I reiterated, "The apple tree.. how do we get there?"

One of them jumped in excitement and began chattering again with the others, and then they directed me to follow. Running, jumping, and flying, they pounced away quickly. I followed.

They were actually quite difficult to keep up with. We continued this for another ten minutes or so, until my newfound friends all came to an abrupt stop. We were not at the tree.

"This isn't the tree," I said, sarcastically, "why did we....."

I then realized why we stopped. There was something else out here with us. And then it emerged from behind the grass. Our eyes interlocked. My little blue eyes, to its big red peepers. The melting skin peeling back, showing its crusty flesh. The long, chainsaw claws hovering in front of it, as if it were praying. A giant mantis stood at least five times higher than myself, and it looked so..... hungry.

This.. indescribably strange, spine tingling shriek screeched loudly as it slashed its deadly limbs about and slicing through the grass like wet paper.

It moved quickly, but was bulky and had to stop to clear paths, that it may chase me. I- *oof!* I felt the wind quickly exert from my chest as I tripped and hit the ground.

Quickly, I turned around, and there it was.. hovering ever so menacingly above me. The ground sizzled as its acid saliva dripped into the dirt, palps twitching. I tucked my head down under my arms as my end drew near.

Thunk
What the-
thunk, thunk

The squirrels stood ever so bravely on a nearby rock, throwing stones at the mantis' head. The attack wasn't enough to do any real damage, of course, but it did distract the oversized insect long enough for me to scurry to my feet. Think, think, think! Aha! One of the pillars of grass was spliced from the rampage, leaving a small sliver hanging loosely. I ran to it and began prying it back and forth. The snapping noise redirected the bug's attention to me. The piece of grass was around four feet long and sturdy as iron. I held the blade with both hands as the mantidae charged once more. Several small stones lay scattered about between he and I. Maybe the mantis was too enraged, or perhaps just dull witted.. but it failed to notice the loose gravel and skid and slipped violently until it... crashed. Falling directly on top of me.

Everything went white, and my head echoed in an ear bleeding ring, like getting hit with a flashbang grenade. In the white abyss, a blood red butterfly fumbled in a fuzzy flutter, and landed on my chest. As my vision slowly cleared, I could make out the three little fluffy silhouettes standing around my head. I came to, and the beast was dead. The grass sword plunged deep into its chest, puncturing its vitals. I, too, had sustained injuries. The acid blood caused second degree burns on my hands, and a part of the grass blade had shattered off and pierced into my pelvis. I could feel the breakage in the bone. It would not be possible for me to walk now. All I could do is lay there and cry. The squirrels tried to comfort me, cuddling my hands and wiping my tears. The little ignorant darlings. My stomach growled loudly again. They sat in silence for a moment, then hopped away in different directions. Abandoned, broken, bleeding, and starving... I may have survived the attack of a huge monster, but the hunger was what had been the underlying bringer of death. Wait.. can I die? I'm already dead.. so what happens if I die here? Do I just continue in torment? Do I go somewhere else? Would I, myself, turn into a butterfly? Wha... and then they returned; sweet squirrels carrying sticks and vines and such, and they began binding them into a pair of make shift crutches for me. My eyes swelled in tears again, but they weren't bad tears. In all of Deadland.. the whole time I was in Canada... I guess it just felt nice to have friends again.

They helped me to me feet. Two of them grabbed me by either shoulder, fluttering their wings to help me walk, whilst the third guided us. And we reached the tree. It was at this moment that I came to the realization that these things hadn't been getting bigger, but, rather, I had become a mere fragment of my stature. I mean, the apples swaying above were gargantuous; they looked like red hot air balloons sitting up there. So, the three critters took hold of me, slowly elevating me towards the treetop. We had to stop a few times and rest between the bark, as their wings got tired. The blood loss was also causing difficulties in me staying conscious. I tried a few times to climb on my own, but only made things more difficult for us all. Nevertheless, we eventually made it to the top. We landed quite roughly in a cleared, flat area. The squirrels rolled and played for a moment; I think that they live here.

With my last bit of strength, I pointed towards the apple and muttered, "Please."

Yet, all seemed to stand still, and my three friends just stood there, staring at me.. in complete silence, save for the light wind whistling around us. The entire atmosphere seemed to nearly freeze in time, and then their cute little buckteeth slowly began curving and folding into dagger-like flesh ripping fangs, and their soft fur turned grimy and coarse. A sickly, low barking sound gurgled under their breath. And then my three friends became seven. Then became ten. The rabid little monsters came crawling out more and more, until I found myself surrounded by about twenty or so of the rabid little monsters. Inching closer and closer, the whole tree rattled with their wicked growling. Closer, and closer. The world began to fade to black. My mind burned with that name again.. Fenrir.. Closer... Alas, I passed out from the trauma.

My parents, the wreck, the rose, the gunshot, the wolf... all such vivid memories flashing before my eyes. I seemed to have such dumb luck with 'surviving' things, even in death, and when I awoke, everything was still okay. I stared at the polished crimson cobblestone ceiling, then... *gasp* I sat straight up in bed. Where the hell am I.? I felt no pain.

I looked under the blanket and, "No wounds." I said aloud. "Did I just dream it all again.?"

"Not a dream, I'm afraid," said an unfamiliar woman's voice.

I turned over to see a beautiful woman dressed in a silky red dress, with fair skin, long blood red hair, and a chiseled ruby crown, holding a small, shiny red apple. She also wore an odd metal contraption on her back.

"No, not a dream at all," she said as she tossed me the apple, "those filthy vermin intended to clean your bones, my dear."

I smelled of burnt hair and blood.

"So.. you saved me?" my words rudely rolled as I talked and took a bite of the apple.

It could've been poisoned, like in the children's fairytale, but I was too hungry to care.

"Thank you. But... who are you?"

Her cherry red lips smirked, "Why, I'm the Velvet Queen."

lightening crackles

My heart sank a little as I recalled the warnings of this woman. This is the wicked woman that Mr. Elmsworth had told me to stay away from her, but.. she can't be that bad, though, right? I mean, she saved my life.. right? She... she's.. The smell of freshly cooked food stole my mind.

"Hungry? Come down stairs, child."

We walked down to the dining room. This castle was huge. Paintings of the Velvet Queen hung on most every wall, and the windows were covered by wolf skin curtains. In the middle of the dining room was a long table, holding as much food as an all you can eat buffet. I sat down, and her servants began making my plate. I didn't say a word to them, yet they gathered for me exactly what I wanted, as if they could read my mind.

"So, Blair, are you enjoying your afterlife in Deadland?"

What kind of a question is that? And how does she know my name?

"Not necessary, madam," I replied, "Everything seems so violent. Although, I do enjoy the scenery."

The food was indescribably delicious.

"Well, things will get better, dear. You just have to find your place. Everyone and everything has a place here."

I cleared my throat and wiped my mouth. I felt like I was going to pop. My body has been healed, my stomach is full, and I'm out of the wilderness.

"You are the ruler here, yes? Basically the goddess of this world?"

She smiled and nodded yes.

"Then are you able to find people? I'm looking for my parents. Jack and Sally, and my boyf-"

"Oh, why.. it's quite possible. But it can prove." her voice grew dark, "difficult. But, yes, I could help you."

She returned to her pleasant self.

Overjoyed at the thought, I replied, "I would be beyond grateful, your highness. And in your debt."

The servants took away the dirty dishes, and the Velvet Queen began to walk away, "Follow me."

I followed her to the throne room. It was just a large, almost empty room with a few large gargoyle statues, two thrones, and an enormous, circular, stained glass window that nearly covered the entire wall. She sat in the larger throne.

"Do you like my castle?" she called, "It's the Velvet Manor."

"I certainly do.. it's quite lovely. And what is it that you were saying about my parents?" She motioned me to sit in the other throne.

"And... what would you say if I told you that you could just stay here?"

I became a bit frustrated, as it seemed she was avoiding the subject, "That's absolutely generous, but, please.. my family and my boyfriend, madam?"

I walk towards the throne, to the steps before them.

"Yes, loved ones. I'm sure we can find room for them. Now come and sit."

I took a few more steps.

"And.. finding them; how do we do it."

The Velvet Queen remained silent, becoming irritated with me, and the room's temperature began to rise dramatically.

"I said sit!"

I stopped, then took a few steps back. Her eyes glowed just like embers and, as she stood, fire rose along the walls, trapping me in this room. I tried to run-

"Seize her!" she shouted, summoning the statues to come to life in crackling flames.

No way out, no way to defend myself, so I just closed my eyes and screamed the first thing that came to mind:

"Fenrir!!!"

pshh! The stained glass window smashed into a million pieces as a huge white wolf came crashing through like a spear of light, knocking over the Velvet Queen and landing in front of me.

"Get on," he snarled.

Without hesitation, I climbed on his large back and he leaped through the shattered window of the Velvet Manor and into the raging red ocean below.

CHAPTER 4

True Friends Lie Underneath

The feel of travelling through the water at such a high speed and the fireballs exploding at the surface of the salty sea was such an adrenaline rush. The wolf swam as gracefully and flawlessly as a dolphin, and, seemingly as fast as a speeding bullet, we plunged deeper into the oceanic abyss. 'I do hope we are nearly wherever it is he us leading us' I thought as my lungs tightened in my chest. Shortly later, we came to the ocean's floor. Fenrir's big paws gently landing on the white sand. We were not alone, either. Bubbles drifted from his mouth, as did it from the rabbit and the others that gathered 'round. But I.. I can't fucking breathe under water. And I can't hold my breath any longer! I.. I.... I...! I fell into a full blown panic attack.

"Blair!" shouted a voice that I seemed to recognize, "Blair! ... Fenrir, help her out real quick."

Fenrir turned and donkey kicked me right in the stomach. I would say he knocked the wind out if me, but.. ya know. The pain was a quick, sharp jab and I instinctively gasped for air.. underwater.. I felt the water shoot down my throat and fill my lungs, and exhale all the same. I was able to breath just fine.. Calming down, I better observed my surroundings. The others gathered at a long wooden table.

The rabbit's twitchy eyes met mine, and he motioned me to sit with him. And I did.

Fenrir then spoke, "Blair, I'm sure you are lost at this point, so allow me to explain: I am Fenrir, the white wolf.

The two provocatively dressed women beside you are Velle and Belle, demon sisters trapped here from Hell, the gloomy figure dressed in black at the end is uh.. well, he hasn't really spoken, but he has been a big help and we just call him Spooky, and this fluff ball beside me is Mr. Dea-"

bonk!

The rabbit smacked Fenrir in the head with his cane, "My name is SIR Death!! Mr. Death was my father... Now, Ms. Blair, we are the Order of Cerulean; a band of rebels set out to take down the Velvet Queen and her vast followers. As I had previously explained it you back in chapter two, souls are no longer able to pass on to heaven and hell, and this is quickly escalating to a problem of colossal, astronomical proportion. I'm talking the complete and utter end of the universe and each realm of the astral plane! And you, oh baby, you are..." he paused, "say, where are the others? Fenrir! Where is the rest of the Order? We're missing, what.. one? Three?"

Fenrir motioned, "No, these two."

And the other two members of the order approached from the distance of the murky sea. A handsome man, and a lovely woman. Tattered clothing and a loving aura. It was my parents. I swam to them and embraced them tightly. We were all at a loss for words. And I know what you're thinking 'she's going to wake up in a few paragraphs because this is just another dream or mirage', but, no. This wasn't a dream or a mirage, or anything of the sort. It was really them. Shackles and broken chains were bound to their wrists and ankles, and one large broken chain protruded from their stomachs. I looked into my mother's tear filled eyes.

"Those chains. Are you the ones that escaped from the Soul Chamber?"

She nodded her head, but didn't speak a word.

"Mother?" She looked down with grimace, her mouth bound shut with translucent crimson threading, as was my father's.

"Sewn shut by deadbinds; a powerful silencing magic known only by the Velvet Queen. It's a type of punishment she uses on anyone that speaks against her and can only be broken by her sorcery, and I'm afraid that may be quite unobtainable, my dear," Sir Death advised me.

At least their safe, I guess.

"So what's next? Why did you bring me here?"

The arrogant rabbit hopped down from the table, "We kill the bitch and set things straight. Here, lemme tell you about the master plan:

In order to break the locks on Heaven and Hell, we must destroy the Velvet Queen's source of power at the core, which will entail taking her out of rule a.k.a. stabbing her repeatedly. There is also some sort of key that unlocks the light of the world and is rumored to be held only by Deadland royalty, so it's off with her head! BUT we can't take her head unless we have the Caesurrex, which is an ancient and powerful sword of mythological legend that may or may not actually exist. And here's the kicker! We must also first destroy the Deathborn, as he is in control of the spiritual stream of this realm and could resurrect the Queen as soon as we've slain her. Any other world and I would have supreme ass kicking skills over him, but each body of Death gets special power and jurisdiction within their particular realm, and he called dibs. Anyways, we kill the Deathborn, vanquish the Queen, destroy the core, and save existence. Not to mention the hordes of minions, booby traps, unspeakable torment, and psychological warfare we will likely encounter. Capiche? We've, erm.. been planning and figuring this out for a while."

Myself and the others remained silent.

Later that night, everyone retired to their homes amongst the array of circus-like tents on the sea bed; mom and dad had one for us. My parents were sound asleep, but I couldn't keep my eyes closed. There was a dim light glowing outside, and my investigation led me to a fireplace. Underwater. That I can breathe in. Nothing in this God damn world makes any fucking sense. Anyways, Sir Death and Belle sat by the fire, and I joined them. Skinless eels circled the campsite in the distance, and their blood shrouded us in a red fog. Something had been bothering me for awhile, though, and this seemed like an appropriate time to ask.

"Sir Death," I inquired, "what exactly happens to a person when they die in Deadland?"

He poked the fire with his stick a few times and replied, "You don't die in Deadland. Generally, your soul would get reevaluated and you'd go into the holding cell (also known as the Soul Chamber) until judgment and, ya know.. you'd go up or down. Though with this being the reason we are all here, as of late, those that meet their fate in Deadland now remain in that holding cell and endure constant torment, all of their life being drained out over and over, fueling the Velvet Queen's malicious scheme. Imagine drowning, until you die, then coming back drowning again from the moment of your resurrection. Very few have ever escaped, but luckily your parents managed to pull it off. Die again, however, and you'll cease to exist; forever faded into the world that never was… the Oblivion."

I nodded and headed back to my tent.

"Blair," I heard him call as I turned away, "I was wrong

about you. This actually.. may not be beyond you, and you may very well be the key to saving us all. There has been an unexpected manifestation."

I turned back to thank him, but he had already left and Belle was asleep in the fire. I made my way back into my tent and began to undress. The candles around me extinguished.

"There's more than one way to kill Deadland royalty."

I jumped at the unsettlingly dark voice. His voice send shivers throughout my body, yet there was an unexplainable sense of comfortability all the same. It was Spooky, floating in the black, dead space. I was paralyzed and speechless.

"Killing her is the only way to take the curse off of your parents, and nobody here even knows if the Caesurrex actually exists. So I have an alternative."

As ominous as he was, I couldn't help but trust him; it was unnatural.

I looked up at him, "H-How, sir? Please tell.. tell me," I stuttered.

Long black tentacles dripped from his black cloak and wrapped around me, lifting me up to him, and he handed me a curvy bladed dagger.

I held the embroidered blade in my hands, "This is a special kind of blade with simple instructions. Plunge it deep into her heart."

"Thank you, Spooky."

He lowered me back down, "My name is Nero, and don't thank me; not yet. We'll just say that you owe me one." And then he disappeared into the dark shadows.

Mom and dad were still asleep. I laid down, and managed to actually get some rest myself. I had such a strange dream. I dreamed that I was standing on the peak on a tall mountain, looking into the face of God in the fading evening sky. The blood ocean was parted, and amongst the sand lay Damien. And it began to rain black broadswords that were engulfed in flames, penetrating his body and vanishing. The water crashed over his corpse and healed his wounds, just so he could be impaled to death again, and repeat. I saw the Velvet Queen approach me with one of the flaming swords, shoving it down my throat and crumbling my body in embers, down to nothing but a broken heart. I was abruptly awoken before dawn by Fenrir howling. Too early. Dad never let me sleep in back home, and this morning was no different. He came in and managed to get me up, and we all met at the table outside. The table was set with a variety of fish and white rice. We sat down for breakfast, and the demonic sisters rushed in to sit by me. They gossiped about surprisingly normal things: favorite foods, complimenting my appearance, relationships.. it reminded me of lunchtime conversation at school.

"So, Damien, huh?" Velle asked, "Tell me about him; how did the two of you meet?"

"Damien.. *heh* well, we met about seven years ago. He was a transfer student that had just moved up to Seattle with his dad from Oregon. He was awkward, and uncomfortable.. just like me. We ended up hitting it off and became good friends. That Valentine's Day he drew me a picture of the two of us holding hands by the sea with a 'Will you be my Valentine? Check yes or no'. I was so damn shy.. and just ran away. That summer he went on vacation with us to the beach. He was standing by the shoreline by himself.. and I walked up and held his hand. And that was the beginning of the best thing in my life."

"Awww, how cute!"

The two of them were something else, but it was nice to reminisce.

Sir Death began his battle plan of the day.

"Alright, everyone listen up. Today is the first day of the rest of our afterlives. Our first priority needs to be fortifying this outpost. We need to be able to defend against any offensive maneuvers, and house an army. Blair, you, your mum, and Velle are going to get a ride to a nearby island and search for food. Jack and Fenrir, start on the barracks. Spooky, you.. you... now where did that sexy goth boy go? Never the matter, let's get started! Belle, I need to speak to you in private.

Velle turned out to be a water demon, being that she could manipulate it and command its creatures. She whistled, and forth came a giant sea turtle large enough for the three of us to ride upon. Shortly later we were at a small island. It was tropical with lots of fruit bearing trees. Velle and I would climb to the top, cut the fruit loose, and drop it to my mother below. Velle had such an enjoyable, playful heart; throwing berries at me and running away, swinging from branches like a monkey, laughing at practically everything. Just like a child wou... like Emma would.

We filled up all the baskets we brought, and it was only mid-day, so we started looking for more useful items to bring back to camp. The island really wasn't very big, but we managed to find a bit of rope, an old rusty pirate sword, and a few wooden planks that had washed ashore. It was all pretty worn and worthless. We headed back to the turtle to return, and the real treasure appeared. A wild boar was grazing nearby.. and it was as big as a horse! It was fat and juicy and needed to be tonight's dinner. We huddled together and devised the perfect plan.

I drew it out in the sand:

"Alright, we tie the rope from this tree to that one. Mom and I will hide there. Velle, you.. you're going to get him to chase you towards us. When he trips on the rope, you and mom pick up the planks and start beating him, then I'll chop into his head with the sword. What do you guys think?"

"I like it!" Velle exclaimed, mom just nodded.

We tied the rope and got everything ready. Mom and I watched as Velle, fearlessly, tiptoed towards the huge animal.

She got right behind it, took in a big breath, and screamed, "Let's go, BIOTCH!!"

and slapped him right on the ass. She darted towards us, laughing hysterically, and he charged behind with steaming anger. She hopped the rope, and his feet made contact with it.. easily snapping right through it. He got to me and I swung the sword as hard as I could.. also a flop, as it snapped and barely even broke skin. Neither mother nor I were fast enough to catch up to them. He chased Velle and gained lead with each passing moment, and she was running out of land. Alas, once her feet hit the sea, she kept running across the surface. About twenty feet out, she stopped and turned to taunt him. He made it only a few feet in before he decided to turn back. And when he did, guess who he saw. Me. Standing there with nowhere to run. His hoof raked at the sand as he lowered his head and readied to charge. Water splashed high when he took off, but he only managed to take one step before stopping again. Velle had him... hogtied.. with some sort of water lasso. She drug him into the water and laughed as she held him under, until all of the bubbles stopped. We loaded everything up onto the turtle and headed back to camp. I am disturbed.

We returned and unloaded our haul.

"Oh, and this," said Velle, cracking open the skull of the sweet turtle that had been such a help, "more meat!"

Belle shook her head. She was obviously used to this kind of behavior. I hadn't gotten the chance to know Belle, but she was easily pegged as the strong silent type, and mature beyond her years. The barracks were nicely framed, and Fenrir was roasting the boar over an open fire. Dinner was like a tea party. Everyone was smiling and acting quite bonkers, except me. I just watched. Mom and dad were laughing so hard they were crying, even if it was muffled. It was simply-

thunk

"Huh?" I thought, as a piece of potato bounced off my head.

"Party pooper!" Velle yelled at me, proceeding to throw another.

Belle shrugged and smiled. Alright... take this! I picked up a banana and held it over my head to throw. Velle just giggled and pointed at it. When I looked up, I saw that she was quickly filling it with water until *POP!* it exploded and a banana mush plopped into my hair. These physics are... fantastic. Everyone seemed to get a pretty good kick out if it, though. I'm sure it was hilarious from an outside perspective. I'll get her back, haha.

"Big sis," Velle asked, all the laughter leaving her voice and looking up, "What's that?"

I turned my attention to see the strange line going across the ocean, making a whooshing sound and seeming to be getting larger... or closer... The sea was parting.

Everyone stood as the waters parted, revealing her maleficence.... the Velvet Queen, whom sat upon a back of a black flaming dragon, accompanied by her serpentine minions.

"Well, well. Roger Rabbit, two demon traitors, a pair of lost souls, a wittle white puppy, and one blue bitch. Quite the posse you have here, I must say. My pets were able to find you rather easily after your brilliant rescue."

The skinless eels made a hissing laughter, circling again.

"Who'd have ever thought you could be so brave, Fenrir? Certainly not Selene."

Fenrir lowered his head and growled.

"Awh, did I hit a nerve, boy? To think, you could've prevented all of this. No matter, you'll all be in my Soul Chamber soon. Now... allow me to give you a little gift: 'I curse the seas, so that you may not breath! Let brew a storm that shall never cease! Unleash the beasts seeking flesh to eat, spread my blight across the land and sea! So mote it be!!' I've tried to be civil, but I think it's high time I stop playing nicely. Enjoy the festivities. Ahhahahaha!"

She crackled her evil laugh and a mighty storm began to rage.

"Fenrir, what did she-"

But he cut me off, "Everybody move! NOW!"

It was too late, though. The water collapsed from the surface to the hundred and fort seven meters down where we were. The table, the tents, everything crashed frantically and swirled harshly. Giant whirlpools were forming left and right, violently scattering everything in every direction. Ancient apex predators rampaged in the chaos. Velle cried for Belle and myself to help. We tried with all our strength to swim to her, but the force of the spell was too great. All we could do is struggle and watch as she was being ripped apart and eaten by the prehistoric looking monsters. Her blood cast potent red clouds, drawing more of them, swarming in to gulp down the various body parts floating in the water. I can't breathe.. I can't swim.... My body convulsed at the pain as my oxygen supply reached its end. I just closed my eyes and let the unforgiving current take me away.

CHAPTER 5

Unleashed

Life is a completely random chain of events that is entirely unpredictable. Just when you think you have it all figured out, everything can change in a mere instance. Death is no different. God. Satan. Heaven. Hell. It's all just the ending of a game that we never asked to play.

> "If there's one thing the history of evolution has taught us, it's that life will not be contained. Life breaks free, it expands to new territories, and crashes through barriers painfully, maybe even dangerously, but, uh, well, there it is."
>
> -Ian Malcolm

Awakening, lying upon a vast, lawless shore. The old beach stretched for as far as my weary eyes could see, and before me lie a jungle, ravenous and evil. There were neither any sign of civilization, nor of my comrades, nor of my parents. I'm alone... again. I pulled myself from the seafoam coffin that had gathered around my battered body and stood to my feet. I looked around a bit to better grasp my situation. Sand, trees, rocks, and a smoking mountain in the distance. Having not the slightest idea of my location, I thought it best to get to high ground.. then perhaps I can come up with a plan. The midday sun beamed against my pale skin as I ventured through the horrendous vegetation. Loud roars and moans echoed in the distance, and flesh craving creatures flashed in the dark of my peripheral vision. No matter. My goal was set and I would not lose focus, though, I must admit, the low hanging hisses and growls were frightening enough to make my spine shiver.

Hours of stealthy venturing passed, and finally I stumbled upon a small waterfall with a nice spring. Thank God. The sea salt and hot sun had me beyond dehydrated, and my skin was burned and splicing. Without thought, I dove into the clear cold water. The coolness and freshness held a rejuvenating property, and the aching of my body seemed to vanish.

splash I emerged from the water.

A drizzle started, its droplets of water sizzling against the rocks surrounding the natural spring. The smell of rain on the water attracted a group of nearly frogs, the largest of which I'd ever seen! They were a heavy green, like a bullfrog, but about four times the size. And their plumb legs *my stomach growled* those legs would make for a hearty meal, indeed. I had to catch at least one of them. I sat upon a large rock and watched them swim. There were three of them, just swimming and playing amongst the lily pads. The rain fell at a moderate pace and had cooled the atmosphere. I grabbed a stick, about an arm's length, and whittled the end of it into a spearhead. I waited until one came into reach, and JAB! I missed.. and it disappeared amongst the rocks. Dammit! The spear wasn't long enough to reach it. I stood up, still determined. Another was swimming nearby. I'll most certainly get this one. I raised the spear above my head and cast with all my might.... missed. This ribbit boy also vanished into the rocks, and now I've lost my gig. Only one left. I grabbed a new stick, carved it sharp, and waited for the final dinner bell to near. As it swam into range, I leaped from the rocks and into the water like some sort of Neanderthal, but the little bastard swam out of my way just in the nick of time and went into hiding amongst the water lilies. I've got him now. I carefully approached the light green pads, cornering him, and *STAB!* ..nothing under the first. I drew my weapon again, *STAB!*, but still, nothing. The tip of my spear was nearly dull now, but I raised it once more and...

THUNK!

I felt it pierce flesh. I ripped the lily pad away and... beheld my spear stuck into the head of that sneaky green frog.. that sneaky green frog that lie dead on the snout of that even sneakier green plesiosauria. It rose its big head up with its long neck as it shook away my spear and dinner, then revealed the other two heads that were still underwater. Fuck me. I tried frantically to escape the spring, but the rain on the rocks had made them too slippery and impossible to climb.

The dinosaur/hydra hybrid peered at me, menacingly, boasting its long, dagger-like teeth. The middle head rose high, and struck like a snake with lightning speed and enough power that large waves formed in the water. I extended my arms, as if I would be able to stop the death ending bite. In that very moment, it felt like time itself stopped. I opened my eyes to see my blood, suspended in the air, and the monsters teeth only slightly stuck in my arms. Time itself had, in fact, actually frozen. The water felt like pillow top mattresses around me. I moved my arms back and away from those intimidating jaws. Pulling myself on top of the water, the entire world exploded into darkness, leaving me in an empty, pitch black space.

I couldn't move, I couldn't speak. All I could do was lay suspended, watching as this strange, radiant light moved in from the distance. It was an enormous blue butterfly. The tattoo on my chest began to glow, as well. The celestial being landed before me and made alien noises in frequencies of which I had never known, but gave me an overwhelming sense of calmness and clarity... of power. And as quickly as it came, its body burst and the energy pulsating within bolted into my vessel like a million lightning strikes all at once. I closed my eyes in awe, and as soon as I opened them, the world quickly reformed around me, and time continue at full pace. My feet were burning a brilliant blue and allowed me to move upon the surface of the water. My wounds had also all healed, and the ice pick still tucked into the belt of my dress transformed into a shiny, indigo colored rapier, and on opposite arm was a templar shield shaped buckler with, well.. you know... rose designs. I could protect myself now. I could fight. The heads took turns striking wildly. The center struck, but I dodged and buried my blade right through its big, ugly eye. The second and third came in for the kill, and my blade was stuck in the skull of the first. I felt the teeth of one digging into my right leg, the the other scrapped against my shield. The bites weren't nearly as effective as I'd imagined. It hurt and I bled, but my body was conditioned a great deal more than before. I ripped my blade from the dinosaur, sloshing brain matter that splattered on the rocks. Dead. Eyes set for number two. The sword began burning with blue fire that intensified more with the more adrenaline that rushed within my veins. I gave two burning strikes to the foul beast's esophagus; clean cuts all the way through. Dead. The magical blade started ringing and vanished, but caused my body itself to swirl in the blue fire. I was storming with power that I never dreamed of possessing. I just grabbed the final head and twisted with all my might, snapping its neck out of socket in a single jerk. The huge beast splashed and fell dead in the water. I had, at this point though, completely overexerted myself, and my body could no longer handle the pressure. With the last of my strength, I climbed atop the vanquished creature and rested. Nap time...

The rain became a heavy downpour as I awoke, gazing in a dead glaze through the treetop canopy to the grey rain clouds. Nightfall was setting in, and I was about to drift back asleep when one of the trees started moving in a most peculiar way. Wait, that's not a tr- *STRIKE!* a fourth head had been lying in wait?! I rolled back into the water just before the bite. What? A fifth? Six heads?? The new heads had not been waiting, but had just recently been grown. Oh, dreadful.. it truly IS a hydra! The six heads danced in mockery. I starting thinking of how I would get out of this one. Maybe if I can somehow trigger that power, I could fight them off.

I had to act fast, "ROSE MYSTIC, ACTIVATE!!" I shouted loudly.

Nothing happened.. the dino-hydra nearly seemed to laugh at my failed attempt.

"Go magic! Blue on! Flower power..?"

This did nothing but make it mock me more so, and I felt like an idiot.

"Flower power? Really?" a voice lightly verbalized from outside of the spring, "You want to keep making a fool of yourself, or is it cool now if I go ahead and take this thing out?"

Belle walked up on the rock beside me and tossed me a vine, "Climb up." I climbed up and she pushed me back, casting fireballs every time the monster attacked.

Her spells were flying everywhere, arrow-like flames came out so quickly that they were buzzing the creature's heads off left and right, until she finally fell to one knee. The heads just kept growing, two in place of each she had destroyed. They opened their mouths and all struck at once. Belle quickly jumped back to her feet and turned her palms to the sixty something oncoming heads.

"Spiritus Ignis!" she screamed in a demonic tone.

Her eyes glowed like white hot metal. The beasty retracted and tossed aimlessly in pain. Large lesions formed on its skin, and smoke bellowed from its mouth and eye sockets as it cooked alive. Even the water evaporated into steam, and the well done dinosaur lay at the bed like a Thanksgiving turkey.

Belle started a fireplace nearby and we set up a small campsite, and found that my sword had reverted back into an ice pick. I'll let you guess what we ate. She was trying hard to keep her calm demeanor, but I could tell just how broken she was by her facial expression.

"So, can all demons control fire?" I asked, trying to strike up some kind of conversation to break the heavy tension.

"I can control it, summon in, and Spiritus Ignis is kind of my specialty move. Takes way too much energy, though. Velle, on the other hand." she couldn't hold those tears back any longer, "...god dammit.."

She quickly wiped them away. I thought back to seeing her getting dismembered during the attack, and started crying again myself.

"I'm so sorry, Belle."

She hugged me tightly and looked into the haunted distance, "We all lost something. Your parents. I know you and Velle were becoming friends."

I thought about Emma, "Yeah, she was a pretty cool

kid. A bit crazy, but pretty damn cool. She reminded me of my little sister, actually. I think she's lost somewhere in this world, too."

"We spent our whole lives losing; our friends, our family, homes, everything. I didn't think death would be so similar."

We told each other tales back and forth most of the night, trying to think about Velle and the others as little as possible. Our hearts needed a break.

"Say, who's Selene?" I asked, remembering the Velvet Queen mentioning the name.

"Selene.. she was one hell of a woman. Smart, gorgeous, and a great warrior. She was Fenrir's old lady," observing the enticed and confused look on my face, she continued, "Oh? You don't know? Fenrir isn't really a wolf. I mean, he is, but he wasn't always. You see, he was set to be the King of Deadland, and was to marry Helena, whom you know as the Velvet Queen. But Fenrir was in love with Selene, a simple farm girl that would take her place as queen if they married. Helena was heartbroken and became furious, and ordered the execution of Selene. She was tied up and tortured in the castle courtyard. Fenrir fought against the entire castle guard, killing dozens of men. But it wasn't enough. Just as he reached his dearly beloved, he was pinned down, his arms broken behind his back, and made to watch as his would've been bride-to-be was brought to one nightmare of a death. The Velvet Queen then banished him from the kingdom, and cursed him to forever appear as a ferocious beast that no woman would ever love again. If she couldn't have him, then neither could anyone else. After that, the queen's bitterness never went away, and she began taking her wrath out on Deadland and all of its inhabitants. Selene's soul was the first to be trapped in the Soul Chamber. Fenrir constantly blames himself and lives with that pain, but anyone would've made that same choice. Love is the bind that traps all souls, yet is the key to set them free."

I couldn't even fathom what I'd been told. The horror and pain that torments his poor heart... and the soul of Selene being trapped. How could someone be so cruel? And then I thought about uncle Cid... the sickness and corruption of humanity. Deadland was no different than earth, really. Sending this red bitch to hell became just as important as saving my family.

Morning light came and we were on our way. Belle thought my idea my idea about getting on top of the mountain was probably the best option. So we headed north, and traveled for nearly a full day.

I thought about the others, and remembered a curiosity I had, "Okay, Belle, so I gotta ask.. what's going on between you and Sir Death?" She blushed and looked away.

"Wait a sec, are you... are you banging a bunny?!"

At this point she burst into laughter.

"Wow, way to keep it subtle, Blair! Haha, I mean.. kind of. He is my lover, but he is actually a very handsome man. He just isn't allowed to show his true form in this world. Something about the Rules of Death. Though, that hasn't stopped him from changing on a few different nights to... *air quotes* 'raise the dead' in me."

My face flushed with embarrassment at the mental image. That's enough curiosity for today.

We had a few more encounters with a few packs of mutated compsognathus, dilophosaurus, and other dinosaurs, but nothing as intense as the plesiosaurus from before. My abilities also seemed to activate of their own free will. It activated each time I found myself in danger, but seemed to need time to recharge between it's emerging. Being this close to the mountain, it was, as expected, an active volcano. We hiked up the warm rock until we reached the summit. Looking across the landscape was like watching a movie based on the Jurassic era meets a syfy horror film. Nothing but oddly colored trees and the angry ocean.

"There's nothing here.. no buildings, no escape, no... Belle?"

Her eyes were focused in the volcano.

"Belle," I called, "what is it?"

But she was completely unresponsive. Rather, she started climbing down, INTO the volcano.

"BELLE!! What in the HELL are you doing?! Belle!!!"

I followed after her. We climbed all the way down, and she continued to walk. I tried to stop her, but it was like she was being drawn to something and couldn't even be budged. Then I saw something odd. In the center of the crust was a totem pole. Various dinosaurs and monsters were carved out, and at the very top was... Velle's severed head.

"What.. the... fuck...." I whispered under my breath.

The ground beneath our feet began to shake and rumble with strange sounds coming from below the surface.

"Belle, I think we should... Belle, we need to go. Now!"

"Just shut up!" she snapped, "My sister's head is on a fucking pike. I-"

crack, pssh, ROAR!

I could hear the rock floor splitting behind us. I turned quickly to see what it was, and beheld a huge fin with black spikes, webbed with molten lava, and the sigil of he Velvet Queen on the side... skimming the volcano's surface like a shark in the ocean. Lava oozed from the crevices it left behind. A colossal spinosaurus finally arose from the core, and several flaming velociraptors followed with him. Belle had climbed up and was casting exploding fire bolts from the top of the totem pole, holding her sister's head.

"Die! You! Sick! Son! Of! A! Bitch!"

She was so furious.. her tears stained black with ash. She screamed and fired and charged at her incendiary foes. The raptors moved quick, dodging left and right. She managed to hit a few of them, but the fire only made them larger. And the firepower had absolutely zero effect on the big boss. Realizing the negative effect, she changed up her strategy by creating a war hammer from the brimstone. She fought so fiercely, and with so much anger. And as heavily as the odds were already stacked against us, now more of the lava monsters were appearing, and the longer they remained on the surface, the larger and more powerful they became. Still, I had to help. My power finally activated and I was able to battle the raptors, but just being near the spinio caused my skin to burn badly.

I finally caught up to Belle, "We're in this together! I will stand by you! I have your back!"

She nodded and we readied in battle position as the piping hot prehistoric army rumbled towards us. Closing in, I noticed one of the raptors get its foot caught in the lava, then trip and fall, getting trampled by the others. Rather than growing, as they did in fire, the lava tore the reptile's foot right off.

"Belle! Did you see that?!"

"I did," she spoke calmly, "I think I know what to do. Blair... thanks for giving Velle a great last day of life, and for being my friend. I hope you find the people you're looking for. Tell Gabrielle. Sir Death.. that I love him, and I'm sorry."

"Belle what the hell are you-"

But before I could finish, she grabbed me by the collar

and looked dead into my eyes as hers began to glow, "Oh, and do me a favor.. kill the bitch."

She then cast me through the air to the top of the volcano, leaving herself surrounded by the enemy. I looked back down at her. She was on her knees, her palms down on the volcanic floor. The molten dinosaurs closed in, and I could read her lips whispering, "Spiritus Ignis."

CHAPTER 6

The Dead Sea

I remember the bright glow of the explosion, and the blast force knocking my body back and ragdoll down the mountainside. I remember the sharp shrills of the dinosaurs as they were being overtaken by the whirlpool of lava, then all of them silencing at once. Belle used her special ability to save me, even knowing that it would send her to the eternal torment of the Soul Chamber... Her words went off like an atom bomb and the volcano erupted. Giant bombs of fire rained down, leaving no mercy as they crashed and ricocheted about the ground, and rivers of lava raced towards the fertile land below. The animals indigenous to the island ran and panicked in fear, but the calamity was too great a force. I couldn't move. The world was a concussive blur. There was no sound now, save for the high pitched ringing in my ears. Although, it didn't take long for me to break the shock and regain consciousness. I've gotta get out of here, and quick! I took off running as fast as I could. Red hot boulders of flaming rock and magma shot from the volcano like meteorites. Craters were being smashed into the ground at random, and the giant beasts were stampeding in every direction, trying to escape as well. The entire jungle was an inferno. Leaping over and crashing through the embered forestry inevitably lead me back to the shoreline. I managed my way through the smoke and ash clouds to the ocean, but now what? I can't swim and just hope to find an island before I drown, but I damn sure can't stay here. The island screamed in pain as a wall of fire swept across its face, disintegrating everything in its path. I have no choice. *splash!* I dove in.

The current was still a rough course, causing me to spiral with the island's debris. Luckily I didn't go too deep. I swam to the surface and climbed onto a floating log and watched the island burn through the thick smoke under the night sky. With my last glance before the smoke became too thick, I could've sworn that I saw Belle standing on the shore. The mind is a truly sick thing for the illusions it plays. I remember closing my teary, stinging eyes, and coughing so much from all the toxins in the air. I remember wanting to give up and just let the sea end me. And I remember those cold hands lifting me from the water and into a small boat. It was my father.

I was glad to have escaped with my life, but everything was simply awful; my father couldn't speak, Belle's gone, and it feels like every bone in my body is broken. We did, eventually, arrive at another small island, with steep shores and a small forest in the center. Fenrir and Sir Death were waiting there.

Sir Death hopped up with a joyous presence, "You actually found her! Ah, Madam Blair! So good to see you! I knew you were alive....ish! And Belle...! Where.. Where is Belle.?"

I wanted to speak, but my mouth was too dry. I needn't say a word, though. The sadness in my eyes must've been enough.

"Tell me she's not.... she.. oh.. oh dear... I, I see."

He did not hop. He did not pounce. Sir Death simply walked away and disappeared.

"Give him time; they were... close." Fenrir said, "Belle and Velle... killed by her intent,"

He looked down, "and your mother is still missing.

We've been searching since the attack, but to no avail. I'm sorry, Blair."

"It's alright," crackled my hoarse voice, "We'll find her, and we'll stop this madness.

Fenrir snarled and shook his head from me, "No. I'm sorry. I should've protected you better. I should've been able to follow you and keep you safe. I won't let you down again."

He licked my cheek and left to help my father with the ship they were building out of logs and vines. By the next night, the ship was complete, and everyone gathered at the fire.. except for Sir Death. Dad was quick to fall asleep. Fenrir kept looking up at me, but evaded eye contact at all costs.

"What's the matter, pup?" I gawked in a playful manner.

"Please don't call me that," he muttered and turned his head from me. It remained silent for a few moments, only the sound of the gentle nighttime ocean waves to be heard.

"I'm sorry... about Selene."

I'd harshly and unintentionally struck a painful kind of nerve, causing Fenrir to become extremely cold and agitated, kicking the fire out with sand.

In the cold dark, he growled, "Don't you EVER say her name again."

I was fearful of his hateful tone, but the pain in his voice is what hurt my heart the most. The wild look in his eyes, like he could kill me at any moment.

"I... I.. I'm sorry," I whispered.

A heard a small sigh of regret exhaled from his mouth, "No, Blair, I'm sorry. It's just that that wound is still fresh. Tell me... where did you hear that name.?"

I went on to tell him everything that Belle had told me, and he added to the story.

"I'm still very... sensitive.. to it," he explained the obvious, "I couldn't protect her, and a hate myself into damnation more and more each day for it. And you... well, you remind me a bit of her. And I just can't bear the thought of losing anyone else."

"Fenrir, I-"

But he disappeared into the pitch black forest, as not to be disturbed. Poor Fenrir... I walked around barefoot for a bit, looking at the stars. I wonder if Damien is out there somewhere, looking at these same stars, thinking about me, too.

That morning, Fenrir had killed and was roasting up some kind of bovine animal, while dad and Sir Death did a final inspection on the boat. We sat in the shade and had breakfast before it was time to go.

Caw, caw! sounded a flock of large birds from above.

"Servants of the Velvet Queen," his black bunny nose twitched when he spoke, "Let's move before she knows where we are."

We set sail as quickly as we could. The sea storm was still pulsing in an angry rage. Sir Death and my father manned the helm and sails, while Fenrir and I waited in the stateroom below. Ever watched a dog ride in the back of a truck? Well, imagine that dog being four hundred lbs. and on rollerblades, and you have Fenrir on a ship. But all jokes aside, this monsoon was absolutely worrisome, and only getting worse. The shifty walls creaked and leaked, but as the hours passed and nightfall took to the world, the waves eventually became less rough against the arc, allowing Fenrir to sit with less bedlam.

All was at a silent standard, until his big white ears twitched, hearing a frightened voice cried from outside.

"Help," plead the broken voice.

He and I rushed to the main deck, and followed the noise to the deck.

"He...lp.." the distraught voice called again as we peered over the side of the ship and into the black sea. Then, there in the silence, a young girl lay unconscious on a small piece of driftwood.

"Dad! Sir Death! Quickly, we need some rope! There a little girl, and she's-"

Sir Death famously interrupted me, "No. We will not stop on this day, nor any other, until that red bitch lays roasted on my dinner table with an apple and a dagger in her mouth. For all we know, this is just another of her traps, and as soon as we bring that abomination aboard, she'll."

splash I dove into the water.

"Dammit, Blair. You demented schizoid of a honey badger! *sigh* Jack, fetch a rope and something that floats!"

I climbed upon the driftwood with the girl and checked her respirations. She's okay. It was far too dark to make out who or what she was, but I heard the rope and a crate splash in the water beside me. I wrapped her arms around my neck, and the others assisted me in getting her aboard our vessel. We made it up and into the light.

"Is she okay?" Fenrir asked.

"Yes, she's fine," I answered, "She's just unconscious. She's... (I turned her face to me) she's.... she's..... my sister..."

My heart pounded as I laid on top of her in disbelief. My father soon joined.

"Take her to the brig," Sir Death rudely blurted, "This could still be a trap, and I'm not taking any chances. So- *oof!*"

Fenrir pounced on top on him.

"Get off of me you filthy, furry, feral, feline hating flea fuck!"

But Fenrir paid him no mind, "Take her to the stateroom," he insisted, "Let her rest in one of the cots, and I'll get her some water for when she awakes."

Sir Death just laid there in a grump. Father and I took Emma downstairs. I climbed onto the cot with her and stayed by her side through the night.

As dawn's new day rose, the sunlight beaming through various crevices woke me. I was a bit dazed, but I could see Emma struggling in night terrors. She was still unconscious, muttering for help and some other things that were unintelligible. Her eye sockets were dark and her skin was flushed.

I put my hand to her forehead, "She's feverish," I said to dad, "Would you get a wet rag for me?"

He got up and went topside. I sat beside my baby sister, thinking of how I'd watched her grow over the years and how protective I always was. I felt so helpless.. so useless.. as she lie there. Footsteps creaked on the wooden stairs behind me. I thought it was my dad, but it was actually Sir Death, and he was carrying the wet rag. He hoped to Emma's bedside and laid it across her forehead.

"There now. That should help with the fever. And... sorry about last night. I'm just so on edge about everything. After what happened to Belle, I-"

I grabbed his little furry paw and interrupted him, "its okay. I understand." He nodded in appreciation and hopped back to man the helm.

The rest of the day proved to be quite uneventful. I remained below deck in case Emma awoke; she never did, but her piping fever had significantly reduced. I also overheard Fenrir and Sir Death talking, saying that there was a hospital where we were going, and that we should be there by morning. The atmosphere seemed to be changing quite drastically and a thick, white fog seeped through the ship's walls, as well. As night befell us, the temperature dropped low enough to where I could see my breath. Dad came down and literally took the shirt off of his back for Emma. He's such a great dad, but I could tell he was beyond distraught with her condition and mom still MIA. He was losing hope. I followed him to the upper level of the ship and discovered that we were sailing through an artic sea. No land in sight, but large sheets of frost and huge icebergs floated about. The wind up here was painful to the touch. My father's skin was quickly losing its natural color.

"Dad, go sit with Emma for a bit; I can help out up here."

His eyes were argumentative, but he gave in after one of my classic 'bitch face' glares. Sir Death was still steering, and Fenrir was using his enhanced vision to guide the ship through the fog. The world was mostly quiet, save for the gentle waves and occasionally cracking of ice.

"Sir Death, veer right," Fenrir advised, "Dammit, further. No, wait, left! Ri-"

"Could you make up your bloody mind??"

"I'm sorry, but it's almost like the icebergs are moving. Wait. I don't think that's an iceberg, it's a-!"

And at precisely that moment a huge shadow began emerging from the fog, followed by the roar of cannon fire. A large cannonball hit Fenrir, knocking him from the bowsprit and smashing him through the ship.

BOOM!

Fired another cannon from behind us, taking out one of our sails. I scurried below to help Fenrir, but the steamy cannonball was hot and scolded my hands. I could smell his fur burning and he had several open fractures protruding from his chest and front leg. Dad rushed to me and motioned for me to go back up, and started trying to move the red hot, steel ball himself. I returned and saw a large vortex cycling amongst the sky, causing the fog to quickly dissipate, which revealed that there were not merely two ships attacking us, but we were surrounded by an entire fleet and they were sailing under the Velvet Queen's flag.

"Hold your fire!" a familiar voice shouted from the largest vessel.

I could hear hooves pounding against the ship's boards, and up stepped the Deathborn.

"This is simple, now. The foolishness has gone on long enough. Hand over the girl and the rest of you will be free to go. Fail to cooperate, and find a watery grave. Playtime is over."

He peered at me with those big red eyes, interlocking with mine. After it was apparent that I wasn't just going to board his ship, he became impatient.

"Alright. Men, ready the cannons," and each of the ships readied each of their cannons at us, "Now I'm going to give you to the count of three to get your sorry dead ass up here, or you're going to have twenty ships with two hundred cannons pulverizing you to a waterlogged mix of blood and dust, and I'll bring the ragged particles of your corpse back to the Queen. So.. Thee. Two. One... FI-"

"Stop!" I interrupted, "I'll go. I'll come with you."

The Deathborn showed his lion-like teeth through a fearsome grin.

"Good girl," he replied.

He then threw down a plank and motioned for me to come. I began walking. The Deathborn was huge. He wrapped his hand around my entire body with ease.

"Finally," he whispered to me, "the little blue bitch is at my disposal. (he squeezed my body tightly and redirected his attention back to our ship) Thank you for your cooperation."

Dad came running back up, his hands burnt to the

bone, carrying Emma from the watery chamber below. The Deathborn looked at him and smirked.

"Watch this," his words growled as he turned my head towards my father, and gave a subtle nod to another ship.

Dad's eyes filled with tears, but before a single move could be made, a large hook attached to a chain harpooned through his chest. He fell to his hands and knees as blood poured onto the floor and my little sister's face beneath him. The chain nearly instantly retracted back to the ship, the sharp hook's barbed end dragging my father back with it. He's… he's really gone.

"No!" I screamed, "You bastard..!"

"What? You didn't ACTUALLY think I was going to let them go, did you? And I'm only getting started."

He dropped me and kicked me to my knees, and pushed my head over the side railing.

"Let this be a lesson to anyone who dare oppose the Velvet Queen. (he cleared his throat) Though I tried to bring this girl back alive, I simply had no choice and had to end her existence in the heat of battle. (he drew his blade to execute) LONG LIVE THE-"

"Over my black furry death lord ass!"

Sir Death jumped to attention with an eight barreled revolving crank cannon that he had stowed away behind the helm, and let out a barrage of cannon fire.

"What the..? FIRE!!" the Deathborn commanded.

And, nearly in slow motion, hundreds of cannon balls blasted towards the ship. Sir Death was shooting the majority of them down before they reached the ship, but some did make it through. Fenrir burst up through one of the holes in the floor, severely injured, yet leaped all the way between the ships and to my rescue, then back to our boat again in the blink of an eye.

"Full sail!"

Sir Death pulled the ropes and we shifted forward with great speed, ramming through anything in our path.

"Blair, steer the ship! Fenrir, you protect Emma! I'll hold them off with my fancy pants cannon!"

The pursuit was on. The enemy ships chased us down vigorously. Their cannons were side mounted and mostly unable to reach us, but our ship was deeply damaged and taking on water fast.

pooth, chink!

The sound of that harpoon firing again. The steel rod slammed through the stern, still dripping with my father's blood. Sinking and unable to move, we were surrounded once again, and this time with no escape. Two ships closed tightly on either side of us, holding us completely immobilized.

"Board that God damn boat, men! Kill the dog and the rabbit, but save the girls for me!"

Beast began jumping from the other ships to ours. Instinctively, my sword, shield, and abilities formed in a blue flash. I was shaking with rage which caused my entire body to be engulfed in a blue flame. The beasts were relentless. Some were fast with long horns, some were tall with six arms. There were many different races, and they seemed endless. We were all so tired, but carried on as a three man army. Hundreds of their bodies lined the ship and sea, and my rose energy finally gave out.

"Alright, enough!" the Deathborn screamed in anger, "Let's end this NOW!"

The two ships holding us in place aimed their cannons down towards our demise. Twenty cannons hung low, readied at our heads. I was hurt and completely out of energy, and Fenrir was practically unconscious when the fight begun due to his prior injuries.

"Fire."

The smell of gunpowder burned my nose, the cannon blast rang in my ears, and the world faded to a wet black.

Dad....

CHAPTER 7

Roses are Blue,
Violets are Dead

Blackness. Odd sounds erring about, like tongues squirming in a dry mouth, or maggots in the skull of a dead child, accompanied by the squeaky rocking of the ship. The voices of our oppressors were a distant muffle.

"Where are we?" I muttered aloud.

Looking more intensely, the darkness surrounding began taking circular.. cylinder forms, and pulsating with an unnatural sway. As my eyes adjusted, I see that they are.. tentacles? Giant black tentacles encasing the entire vessel, blocking out ship from the outside world. What in the heavens is this? No matter how or what, they had shielded us from the attack.

"When I lower my tentacles, its full sail ahead," the deep, spooky voice bellowed.

We all waited in silence, all completely lost at the situation.

"Guess we don't have much of a choice but to trust... it," Fenrir said quietly. I nodded my head and waited.

Moments later, "Now!" the voice roared, and the tentacles swarmed away, slamming into the enemy ships and causing significant damage to the bodies and sails.

We set out full throttle and managed to slip through the chaos. The Deathborn screamed in fury, but the devastating sea assault didn't let up. I kept my eyes forward and smile for a moment at the. Awful sounds crashed and splashed behind us, and as we passed into safer waters, I looked back to see the ending carnage, just in time to see Nero pulling the ships to a watery grave. He had saved us and destroyed the Velvet Queen's armada, and devoured each crew member.. save for the Deathborn, whom abandoned his ship mates into a fiery portal.

Though we had managed to escape the battle, the loss endured left my heart sunken with the ships. Sir Death fashioned a small memorial raft in honor of my father. We filled it with any kindling we could find, then I ignited it and placed the necklace he'd given me for my birthday within the flames, and pushed the small raft to sea. As it floated away and I said my goodbyes, Emma's dreary little eyes slowly fluttered open.

"B.. Blai.. r? Big sister..?!" she spoke, "I was so scarred.. where are we? Where are mommy and daddy?"

I looked back up at pyre disappearing into the fog and couldn't handle telling her the awful truth quite yet.. how mom was gone and our father had just traded his life for hers... "I don't know, sweetie. I don't know."

The ship, though we'd patched it the best we could, was still rapidly taking on water, forcing a crash landing at the first island we came across.

"The Planes of Sin," Sir Death observed, "Not somewhere I hoped to become a part of this journey. The good news is that the Velvet Dominion isn't far from the other side, the bad news is that this may very well be the most terrifying and dangerous place in all of Deadland. We must tread carefully, lest we will not make it through."

I leaped from the deck and onto the shore. As soon as my feet touched the ground, I was overcome with a harrowing sense of impending doom. The very presence of this place shook me to the core. It was too still, and I felt afraid to even speak. The others followed and we proceeded into Sin; Emma rode on Fenrir's back. The atmosphere was so different here. Things were obscure and disorienting, and it constantly felt as if wicked eyes were watching my every move.

We stumbled upon a small, quaint village that appeared to be abandoned.

"Hello?" I called out.

But nothing. It became obvious that there was no one else here. Not a single soul in any of the houses, and the open doors and broken windows indicated that they likely hadn't been occupied for some time.

"Be careful.. I don't like this." Sir Death said in a worrisome tone.

I decided to scavenge a bit but any trace of food or useful items seemed to lay in ruin. That is, until I came to the last house. The door was intact and none of the windows were busted. Unlocked. I opened the door. It was still quite simple. The front room had a few book shelves and chairs, but in the kitchen is where I found the most curiosity. A long buffet table. Turkey, vegetables, bread, pies, spicy peppers.. it was just full of freshly cooked, mouthwatering foods. Though every fiber in my body was screaming for me to turn back, I couldn't. I just couldn't. I gathered the others and we all sat down and began stuffing our faces like wild animals on a fresh kill. I hardly even had to chew because of how tender it all was.

We've all been through so much, and I can't even imagine what's been going through Emma's innocent little mind. I mean, she's just a little kid. Her smile is enough to make my worry go away, though. It's like just seeing her happy takes away all the hardships. The way she crinkles her little nose when her dimples show. The light that burns in those big eyes. And while I observed that innocent smile, I noticed something strange stuck in her teeth. It was moving.

I looked down at the table and instantly began throwing up in a violent heave.

"Spit it out! Everyone stop fucking eating, now!"

The irresistible food we had been enjoying was teaming with maggots. They grotesquely pulsated throughout the meats and squirmed in the pies. Thousands of them. I could feel them churning in my stomach, eating at my insides. The room quickly began to rot and decay and a sinister laughter echoed all around.

"What the hell is this?!" I screamed in pain.

Everyone began spitting and raking the pusy maggot guts off of their tongues. The pain was terribly intense. The walls began to pivot and contort in a rapid, circular motion. I tried to speak, but each time a word would make its way out, so did more bloody vomit. I had to figure something out, and quick, before the little bastards damaged something vital. But what? What could we...! Aha! The peppers! I started shoveling them down my throat. My eyes burst in tears, my skin dripped with sweat, and my insides were on fire. The others followed my lead, and shortly later the larvae were no more. Alas, even with the tiny terrors gone, the room was still in a psychedelic spin, and the faster it spun, the louder and higher pitched the laughter became. Faster, louder, faster, louder, faster, louder, until I just couldn't take it anymore and then... it stopped.

The room, the table, the house, the noise... it all vanished. It's like we teleported to a new place. Reality seemed stable again, like I had just come down off of a bad trip.

"What was that..?" Fenrir panted.

"One of the effects of this place, I presume," answered Sir Death, "This place derived of pure evil. It is as perilous as it is unpredictable. We have to be more alert. We must be more resilient to its trickery. We must.. we must.... we... mus......."

A haunting voice echoed his name in the distance, causing him to slur and lose focus completely. He said not a word, but began hopping in its direction. I called for him, but he would not respond. The terrain was hot and smoky, and the rock landscape smelled of sulfur. The smog was thick and brown, and hurt my eyes and throat. The little black bunny was moving quite quickly, but we followed as fast as we could.

The voice echoed louder.. a woman's voice, "Sir Death.. Sir Death.. help me, Gabrielle..."

A familiar sound with a captivating tone. When we finally breached the smoke, Sir Death stood there motionless, hardly even breathing. And standing before him was a fiery silhouette of a ghostly, ghastly woman. It was Belle.. or at least an illusive representation that looked and sounded like her.

"Come to me, Gabrielle. I've returned for you, darling. Let love embrace yet again."

Slowly he hopped to her, his eyes void of consciousness; memorized in a deep trance like state.

"Sir Death, this doesn't feel right.. I watched her die... You need to snap out of it! Sir Death!!"

But it was no use. She picked him up and brought him to her breast, embracing him tightly.. She grinned with a grim glow, and her eyes intensified with maleficent flames.

"No!"

Fenrir lunged to snatch him from the demons clasp, but was repelled by a force-like barrier. It was too late.

The deceitful harlot's hot breath harshly whispered, "Spiritus Ignis."

The entire field burst into a hell storm of roaring fire, knocking Fenrir, Emma, and myself back with the powerfully hot blast. Sir Death convulsed in her arms. His hair sizzled and fried, his flesh was smoking and splitting, and blood boiled from his mouth, but he put no effort into escaping the demon's clasp. The fire was so great of a force that none of us could even get close to him without badly burning ourselves. All we could do was cry and plead for him to snap out of it. It was useless. We were useless. I... I'm useless.

And as we watched our friend suffer, his little bunny lips gurgled through the boiling bloody foam, "I... I.. love you... Belle."

His last words dropped heavily as his body fell to ash and bone. Sir Death perished with a broken heart.

"You bitch!" I screamed and took off running at her as fast as I could.

"Big sister, no!" Emma cried.

Her words grasped my heart, but the vengeance driving me would not subside. And then it happened. The blue armor, the sword, the shield, everything burst into action and not even the inferno could stop me. The demoness began hurling fireballs at me, but my shield would not be so easily penetrated.

"He was my friend! You sick bitch!"

My war call shook the ground as my sword sliced across her stomach and chest. The wound cut deep, yet almost instantaneously regenerated in a deep red light.

"Foolish little girl," she gawked, "I am the demon known as Wrath. You cannot defeat me."

Her long arms reached out and shattered through my shield like a hammer to a lightbulb. I could hear Emma and Fenrir calling from behind. Her boney fingers clinched tightly around my neck and she lifted me above her head.

The vortex of fire was making my skin peel, and her evil voice whipped against my ear,

"You are going to die, my dear. But before you do, you're going to watch as I damn your sister's soul into Oblivion."

She turned me around and pointed her other arm towards Emma.

"Learn true agony," she laughed and sent a huge beam of bright red light towards my little sister that ripped the very ground as it passed over.

I couldn't speak, and my struggle was useless. The reflection of the blast grew brighter and brighter in Emma's eyes the closer it got. Then it breached the surface of the flame barrier and exploded around her like a missile.

"Emma.." I choked on my own tears.

Wrath's laughter echoed like thunder. She dropped me and I hit the ground with dead weight. Even in my blue state of being, this fire was smothering me.

Panting heavily, I stood to my feet, "You killed my friends, you killed my only sister, now I'm going to kill-"

She kicked me swiftly in the ribs, knocking me down onto my back and hovered above me.

"Insolent little fool.... When will you learn your place? You are but a candle to the Demon of Flame. I am one of the Seven Deadly, and you are nothing but a useless little brat. Your friends are dead. Your family is dead. Even your boyfriend's death... it was all your fault. You are too weak to save anyone," her foot slammed into my ribcage again, "and now, you'll join everyone you've let down."

She pushed her foot down, cracking my ribs. Life began to fade completely. The blue armor and sword shattered, and the world dripped into white. I felt no pain. And as each shard of my gear floated away, the ones above turned to slowly fluttering butterflies, and those below grew into bright blue roses.

"Don't give up."

I came back to. My ribs snapped back into place and I fell upward to my feet. The flames no longer burned my skin, and the butterfly wings and rose petals still surrounded me. Wrath gasped in confusion.

"What the hell is this?!" she asked in panic.

I felt possessed, almost. My thoughts and actions were naturally being manipulated by another force, yet by myself as well.

"I am Blair Sterling, and I have a purpose for being here. You are amongst the wicked of this plane and I am here to punish you for your crimes against the world. I will avenge my friends, I will save my family, and I will be reunited with the boy whom I love. And no malicious spirit nor evil tyrant is going to stop me. I am not useless, and you will not get in my way. This is where our battle ends, demon filth."

The blue swirled in circles at lightning speeds, extinguishing the flames. Wrath screamed and struggled, but was ripped apart piece by bloody piece, swirling in ribbons of flesh, until she was nothing but a burnt scar on the rocky surface. The smoke faded to reveal Fenrir and Emma curled up safely in a ball of light. Someone was watching over us. Needless to say, I was beyond glad to see the two of them. The rose petals hadn't left me, either. In fact, they continued to flutter about and mended all of my wounds. I could control it now.. the power. I picked up the remains of Sir Death and placed them in my satchel to bury him later, and ran to Emma and Fenrir. We embraced in a silent hug of relief and mourning, and closed our eyes.

Shortly later, I opened my eyes to see that our location had mysteriously changed again. The trees, the sun... it all seemed so familiar. Such a strong sense of deja vu.. I looked down, and that's when I realized exactly where we were. There was a stone pile at my feet; a pile of petrified tree. It was Mr. Elmsworth, and we were in the forest where my story here had begun. I had no idea which way to go. But.. the trees! Maybe they could tell me.

"Excuse me? Erumm.. forest? It's me again, Blair. Could you help me, please?"

But there was no response. I could see one's face, asleep, but as I placed my hand on her cheek to awaken her.... cold. A stronger moonlight beamed through, revealing the whole forest had been turned to cold, petrified stone. My observation of the graveyard was cut away by a man's voice shouting from the distance.

"Hey you! Come help me, please!" He sounded distressed, but I wasn't about to let my guard down for a second.

We approached with caution and found man with a compound fracture in his right femur and a bloody shoulder.

"Please, miss, you gotta help me! Those monsters attacked so I climbed this tree.. but after I passed out I fell and broke my leg. My name is Brad; my wife, Lisa, and my daughter are waiting for me to bring food back to our cabin, not far from here," he looked around frightfully, "They'll be back soon.. please... please help me."

It was dark out, and I certainly didn't want Emma exposed to whatever is out here. A cabin sounds a lot safer.

"Alright, we'll help you. But if you try anything funny, my friend over there is going to rip you in half," (Fenrir looked at him, growling loudly), "So, which way?"

He lifted his hand and pointed his finger to the left and assured us he had no intention of causing any trouble, and we began to walk. It was a really grim trip to the cabin. The dark sky hanging dimly over a dead forest that was once so vibrant with colorful life. Nevertheless, we made it to the cabin. "Daddy!" a little voice cried from the window,

"Mommy, look! Daddy's back!"

We helped him inside and locked the door behind us.

"Lillah, go play," Lisa said, looking at her husband's shoulder.

She tended to his wounds and put a pot of stew on the fire while their daughter and Emma played with her toys. Fenrir and I kept to ourselves by the fire, cautiously observing. It was impossible to determine what I should believe or who I should trust anymore. The stew finished, and Lisa had patched Brad up pretty well. We sat down to eat, and he told us stories about his family, and how they'd been surviving here for the last six years. I only caught segments of what he was saying. I'm still worried about my mother, and there has been no sign of Damien since I got here.. I picked at the food, and went to bed. We leave at dawn.

crunch, crunch, crunch

A strange noise woke me from my sleep.

crunch, crunch

It's very dark, but I can see Fenrir asleep by the fireplace.

crunch, rip

Emma and Lillah are asleep in bed..

gurgle, crunch, moan

"What the hell..?"

I lit a small lantern, and there he was. Brad... His eyes glazed over, fleshy lesions in his skin, tearing off pieces of Lisa with his infectious teeth. I remember them now.

The monsters. The undead that walked the forest the night after I first encountered the Deathborn. The bite on Brad's shoulder was a zombie bite, and he had turned!

"Emma, Fenrir, Lillah, get up!!"

I screamed loud enough that they all woke up, and Brad stumbled towards me on his hands and knees, ravenously.

I drew my sword and swung for his head, "Daddy, no!" Lillah screamed through tears.

Contact. My sword dropped heavily with blood. But.. the moans continued. Little Lillah embraced her father tightly, his teeth gnawing at her arm, and my blade protruding through her skull. Her six year old corpse fell dead on the floor, life ended by.. by my hand. Her father showed no mercy and immediately began tearing out and eating her intestines. I was completely paralyzed in shock and guilt.

moovaan, aaahhrr!

Lisa stumbled up to her feet and lunged at Emma.

"NO!" Fenrir roared and pounced on top of them, tearing Lisa's head from her shoulders with his big claws.

The world was mute for me, though. I watched Fenrir re-kill Lisa, then Brad, and then Lillah. I heard the windows shattering and the undead reaching through, as they had been drawn to all the commotion. Still, I was far from myself. The door caved in, and the zombies rushed inside. I whited out.

Hours later, I fell back to reality. I felt so nauseous.. and Fenrir and Emma were watching me with worry and sorrow in their eyes.

"Guys.. what... where are we?" I asked.

"The Velvet Dominion," Fenrir stated, "I, um.. I

managed to get us out after the undead attacked. The castle isn't far from here, but..."

He looked down into the campfire. He was openly crying.

"But what? What is it..?" I asked, though he couldn't even answer me.

"Emma...?" I started shaking in fear, "What's going on?"

Tears streamed slowly down her little cheeks, and she softly whimpered,

"Lis.. Li.... Lisa.." she replied.

I stared at her with more confusion and worry that I'd ever known, until she slowly lifted her shirt.. to reveal... a bite mark.

CHAPTER 8

Till Death Do Us Part

I gave Emma mercy that night, and we buried her the next morning amongst some wildflowers in the green valley below, under a tall willow tree. I spoke of our lives together and of her kind heart, Fenrir said how brave she was. I took a few sticks and a ribbon from my dress and made her a cross, then laid a few of the flowers on her grave.

"Fenrir, I need some time to myself."

He nodded his head, "I'll come back in about an hour. Meet you here," and then left away into the woods.

I sat beside Emma, "I'm so sorry, baby girl. I should've been able to help you. I let everyone down. And you.. I couldn't save you."

I noticed a piece of glass from the cabin stuck in my satchel.

"Hey, Emma. Remember the creek at the park back home? Back when mom and dad were fighting a lot and we thought they were going to get a divorce? You were scared because you thought mom was going to take you away and dad was going to take me.. I told you that I would never leave you, and then we made a promise that we would always be together, no matter what? Right? Well.. I'm not making this an exception. I want to be where you are."

I took the glass in my right hand and placed it on my left wrist. The sharp edge felt like such a relief as I slowly began to relinquish all of my worries. I could hear as my skin split, it sounded crisp.. like tearing damp paper. The warm blood tickled as it trickled down my arm and dripped from my elbow. Such a pretty red.. Everything was becoming colder and lighter.

"Blair!" a sweet puppy's voice echoed frantically from afar.

You're too late, my dear sir. I laid back onto my sister's grave and closed my eyes. Sweet aroma, sweet release.

"Death is not the greatest loss in life.
The greatest loss is what dies inside us
while we live." -Norman Cousins

The nearly magical experience came to a haunting, screeching halt. My heartbeat echoed in my head, and the air became far too dull and dry.. and there is so very little oxygen.. Insufferable. The blank world, the shades of textureless gray and black.. These chains around my wrists.. they simply fade off into the Oblivion. The atmosphere is a torment in itself, causing my entire body to sting like a deep chemical burn. This is not the afterlife I had anticipated.

"Emma?"

I tried hard calling her name, but was only able to emit a small whine. The power of the rose was gone, too. My feet hovered above the ground in a ghostly fashion. I began to wonder about, floating through the empty space, looking for something... anything. Pieces of flesh would fall right off the bone due to the corrosive air, but grow back instantly, only to repeat the same torment. There was nothing here.

jingle my chains subtly shook.

"Huh?"

jingle, jingle is something moving them from the other end? I tried pulling them towards me, but they wouldn't budge a bit.

Until... *jingle, SLAM!*

The chains quickly began retracting, snapping my wrists and pulling my arms out of their sockets by the supernatural force. I was being hurled through the air at hyper speeds, slamming against the ground at times and getting severe road rash largely throughout my body. Something finally came to form other than the teeming darkness. There were these two bright, circular lights, and my chains were going through them. I was drug faster and faster towards it until I finally collided head first and... was sitting in the backseat of dad's car? He and mom were up front, listening to Sinatra, Emma looking out the window, and Damien asleep on my shoulder. What in the world....? I watched dad drive as we approached the curve where we had gone off the road, and I could see the tree where we crashed. But.. we drove right passed it without skipping a beat. I feel so groggy... like I've just awoken from a long sleep. Awhile later, we pulled up to Velma and Cid's house. They were excited to see us, and rushed us inside. The table was set with pizzas and soda, and the house was so warm. Aunt Velma must have eaten a whole pizza by herself, and Cid hadn't been drinking at all. After dinner, Dad turned on the tv and started watching basketball with Cid and mom; OKC Thunder versus Washington Wizards.. I quickly rushed outside. I needed to breathe. The shed was the first thing that caught my eye. It had been converted into a nice little guest house, and Cid had that Chevrolet fixed up like new, parked in the garage. The barn had been painted bright blue and was now housing horses. And the garden... gone entirely. What is going on....?

The next day proceeded as a normal day on earth would. Cid hoped in the Chevy and left for work early and Velma made us all breakfast. Mom helped clean up while Emma drug Damien and I outside for a snowball fight. I've never heard her laugh so much. By lunch time, the three of us were about frozen. We went inside for some hot tomato soup and cheesy toast. Though I was still suspicious of it all, it was kind of hard to question it. I wanted it to be real.. And even if it's not, I think I could be happy pretending. Cid came home that afternoon and asked if I wanted to go with him to town to rent a movie. My heart beat faster as memories of trauma in the barn and garden became more vivid, but the beginning of my panic attack was broken by my dad's voice,

"Go on, Blair. You always pick great movies. Get us something good!" He chuckled and smiled, and I got in the truck.. against my better judgment.

It was about a fifteen minute drive to town. My uncle told me about how he and Velma had met on a fishing expedition, and that he proposed in the back of this truck at a drive in movie theater. Just.. normal conversation. We got to the video store, and I found one of my all-time favorite movies, 'The Labyrinth.' Yeah.. that's the one. We left the movie gallery and went to the general goods store on Main Street. I waited in the truck while Cid ran inside for some farming supplies.

We got home and everyone was hanging out in the living room. Damien was pretty quiet, as usual, but everyone else was laughing and having a good time playing Uno. The cozy fire blanketed the whole room with a gentle orange glow, and the scent of warm vanilla filled the air. It was nice seeing my family so happy. I sat down by Damien and held his hand. He smiled softly and held mine back. Dad won the game and proceeded with his ever embarrassing victory dance, then we grabbed some kettle corn popcorn and turned on the movie. Aunt Velma had never seen it before.

As soon as the movie was over, "Wow, that was excellent!" she exclaimed, "The acting was wonderful, the story was brilliant, and that Goblin King was a real hunk!"

Cid rolled his eyes as she raved, "And the labyrinth reminds me a lot of my garden, *yawn* but I think it's time we're off to bed now, dears. C'mon, Cid, let's go. Goodnight all, I love you."

She blew me a kiss and then the two of them proceeded upstairs to their bedroom. Mom, dad, and Emma went out to the guest house, and Damien and I passed out on the couch watching Animal Planet. 'Garden,' I wondered..

I awoke to the smell of boiling coffee and the sound of crackling bacon. Mom brought me a cup and a plate, along with a bowl of white rice.

"Babe, let's go on a walk after breakfast," insisted Damien, "just the two of us."

Mom gave him a rather wicked look and an odd tension grew about.

"Sure," I replied, "that sounds nice."

Mom got pissed off and stormed out of the room. She's always been a bit overprotective of me, but I'm old enough to make my own decisions, and she hasn't had a problem with Damien since we first got together..

"Blair," she demanded from the other room, "come here please. Now."

Geez, talk about moody. I smiled at Damien and went into the other room.

"You don't need to be going off alone with that boy," there was an angry panic in her voice, "I'm not going to have any daughter of mine get taken advantage of by some bum." I slammed the door so Damien wouldn't hear.

"What the fuck mom?! What the hell are you talking about? You know damn well he's not trying to take advantage of me. We've been saving ourselves for seven god damn years!"

She had never spoken to me like that before. She went on to aggressively badger Damien, but I just turned and left, rather than entertaining the idiocrasy. Damien followed me outside. I walked into the garden to try to clear my head. What the hell was wrong with her? I felt hated. I felt small. I felt insignificant. I felt... I f.... I... the garden? I'm.. I'm in the garden.

"Babe, talk to me. Babe?"

But I could pay him no mind. Everything is too surreal. I took off running.

"Blair, wait!"

But I just ran with Damien chased after me. Through the twists and turns, I followed the path to the best of my memory. And there I found myself at a small tree, about ten feet tall, with mondo grass and black foliage. But... the blue rose was gone. I fell to my knees and my tears poured like rain. Damien finally caught up to me.

"Baby, what's wrong? What can I do to help?"

Then he reached down to wrap his arms around me.

"Just shut up!" I yelled, "You're not real, none of this is real!"

"Blair, what are you talking about? Of course this is real. Just calm down, babe. Okay?"

He tried again to hold and comfort me, but I pushed him away and ran back towards the house. No matter how much I want this, I was wrong. I can't do it. Everyone I love is dead and suffering, and I can't ignore that fact. This world is just a twisted illusion. I decided I was going to run away. Even if I am stuck here, I can't become a part of this beautiful lie. I got back to the house and gathered a few things, and headed towards the barn to take one of the horses.

A final thought on the incident crossed my mind as I entered the barn, 'If this world was set to be such a perfect illusion, then why would it have my mother act so heartless?' Then it dawned on me.. What if she was trying to warn me..? What if that's not Damien..? What if she had found a way to communicate with me and was trying to tell me something about him without him catching on. Or.. since there is a chance of everyone dying and coming to this place.. what if that really IS my family back there? I think I need to get some distance to think everything over and see if I can actually make sense of all these illusive happenings. I turned on the light and the inside of the barn was as new and nice as the outside. The horses were large and restful, silent in their stables. I picked the one I'd take and began to unfasten the gate when I heard the barn door open and close behind me.

"Blair," Damien's low voice resonated, "What is going on with you? You're being-"

"Who are you?!" I cut him off, "Stay away from me!" He took a few steps towards me and I reached for the ice pick.

"Blair, you need to calm down, babe. It's me, okay?"

He kept coming. My heart beat as my fear and adrenaline increased. I... I won't let these liars, monsters, and demons torment me anymore!

"LIAR!" I screamed and darted at him with the pick in my hand, plunging it into his stomach.

"B..Blair..." he coughed, "W... wh.. why?"

He stumbled backwards with the sharp rod still impaling his abdomen. All of the sudden, the lights began fading dimmer and dimmer, until the room was pitch black.

"Such a smart girl, just like mommy," my mother's voice whispered around me in the darkness.

"And so strong, just like daddy," I heard my father say.

Then Emma's little voice shook the ground beneath my feet, "I'm so happy you played with us. You did just as we had hoped, big sister."

What is this? What have I done? My mind warped in an antagonizing schizophrenic abashment as the voices swirled around me.

"Pretty young girls shouldn't be out here all alone.. vulnerable. There's bad stuff out here. Could get hurt," all of the other voices had ceased, "Could get real hurt."

The lights buzzed on in a dim flicker. The room was now run down and visually deteriorating, and that old Chevrolet pickup truck was parked, rusted up with busted windows. I felt uncle Cid's hand wrap in my hair, then forcing me forward and slamming my head down on the hood of his truck.

"Look up there," he said, turning my head to the left.

It was Damien, chains around his wrists and hanging on the wall.

"You made a mistake, Blair. That WAS the real Damien, and now he's gonna die here in the Soul Chamber, causing his soul to disappear into Oblivion with rest of your family. And you are to blame. Haha! You've damned everyone you tried to save. And I am going to enjoy personally killing you.. But first... first we're gonna finish what we started."

And he vanished, his last words still hanging in the air. Damien! I ran to him and stacked a few nearby hay bells to climb up. I tried so hard to remove the shackles or loosen the chains, but they wouldn't budge at all.

"Blai..r.. ru... run.." his voice faintly muttered, "be.. behind you.."

I turned quickly to see a very large man standing on the other side of the truck. My body trembled in fear and doom. Muscular, standing about eight feet tall, wearing nothing but a black sack mask on his head and the sigil of the Velvet Queen tattooed on his chest, with pale.. veiny skin, holding a long, rusty saw blade. My brain rapidly started scanning through anything I could possibly think of to get us out of this situation.

"I won't leave you, Damien. I'll get us out of this, I promise."

The monster of a man started walking towards us. Think... think..... He got closer, about half way between the truck and I. Fuck! I need an idea! Closer, reaching out for me. The ice pick! Regardless of where I am, the power of the blue rose is within me, and that pick is what becomes the sword! I have to do this. I will save us! I grabbed its handle and pulled it from his tender gut, closed my eyes, and focused all of my energy into it, and...

heh, heh, heh

The giant man laughed hauntingly from behind his mask as he grabbed me and tossed me across the room like a child's doll, denting the truck when I collided with it. Chains flung out of the barn walls, wrapping tightly around my wrists and jerking me harshly into a 'T' formation. I was facing Damien, our eyes grimly interlocking as they filled with tears. The monster's cold fingertips raced under my clothing, invading me in ways that crushed my very being. He moved his hand to my waist, and pulled my underwear to the side until they tore, and he cast them to the dirt floor.

"Please, God... please do something.."

But there was only more silence. His large hand slid up my back, and my neck, and covered my mouth, and he.. he proceeded to rape me in front of the only man I had ever loved. All but unconscious, I watched Damien's heart and soul obliterate through his sorrowful eyes as he was forced to watch all the innocence and sanctity I had left be stolen away from me. The putrid assault lasted for what seemed like an eternity, and the creature finally finished performing his horrific act, filling my violated body, leaving me dripping with blood and filth. Trembling, I looked back to my dear Damien as the last of the life he had left his bloody body. The life that I had taken from him.. The abomination picked up his serrated blade from the ground, placed it across my collar bone, and began to slowly drag it back and forth, as to saw my torso in half. The pain of having skin and flesh stripped from the bone was excruciating, but I couldn't care. I didn't cry or scream. I wanted it to happen.. I wanted to stop existing. The last piece of myself had just been ground to nothing. I am nothing but a whore.. used goods. I hung my head and closed my eyes; I'm fucking done.

I could feel the vibrations of my soul becoming erratic, like driving a small plane going through a thunderstorm. I was depleting, dissimulating into Oblivion.

An ignorant little voice cried from the back of my mind, "No, don't give up.."

All this, and part of me is still stupid enough to look for hope. Give it a rest.

"Don't give up," the voice got louder, and deeper, "Blair, please don't give up!"

That voice sounded like... Was that.. Damien? Or maybe... Fenrir? Who-

"Open your eyes!"

I snapped back into reality to see Damien's corpse illuminating. The monster stumbled back a few steps from the growing light. He was like an angel. The bright light burned from his chest and the room shook with howling vibrations, and out lunged that giant artic wolf.. burning brilliantly with a pulsating white. He looked me in the eyes and telepathically spoke.

"None of us have ever blamed you, not once. All you've ever did was try to save us, and now it's my turn to save you... babe."

He then looked the monster dead in the eye, and released an ear shattering howl that disintegrating its body entirely and engulfing the world around me in his same, holy white light. Reality shook and spiraled chaotically. 'Babe,' I pondered, just before succumbing to the exhaustion.

CHAPTER 9

Scena Finis

"We shall go our way into battle . . And we shall be accompanied by the spirit of millions of our martyrs, our ancestors tortured and burned for their faith, our murdered fathers and butchered mothers, our murdered brothers and strangled children. And in this battle we shall break the enemy and bring salvation to our people, tried in the furnace of persecution, thirsting only for freedom, for righteousness, and for justice."
-Menachem Begin, Nineteen Forty-Eight

Characteristics of the world slowly sketched about, showing outlines of the trees and sky, raining, and that glowing white wolf stood above me, looking down, as if I were but a baby in the manger. All came to materialize, and I was lying there in Deadland, atop of my sister's grave with Fenrir crying overhead. 'Was it all just a dream?' I wondered as the blurry world veered into focus. That is, until I felt the tearing pain between my legs and saw the blood staining my thighs. I didn't even want to be saved.. My wrist was no longer bleeding, but my suicide left me with large scars, and the shackles of the Soul Chamber were tightly fastened around my wrists.

"I was so afraid I'd lost you," Fenrir said.

And after a long pause, with no sound but the whistling wind, "You did," I replied in heavy grimace.

He noticed the bleeding between my legs and all the hair on his body stood straight up as he shook lividly. He knew what it was..

We headed north, into the mountains. Both our hearts were filled with scorn and vengeance as we crossed the ridged landscape.

"I smell something," said Fenrir.

"What is it?" I asked.

"It smells like.. blood. Burning blood."

He put his nose high and sniffed a bit more, and around the next bend a bloody trail drug through the valley. It was crusty and coagulated, but highly visible all over the ground and rocky ridges. The further we followed, the thicker it became, housing particles of intestines and organ tissue. We reached a large dome like clearing amongst the dark brown rock to find the disturbing trail to be leading to the source, and there she was... my mother. Her hands and feet tightly nailed to a dogwood cross in the center of the clearing, with her stomach torn open and insides wrapping around the wooden beams. Her eyes sewn open and void of moisture, and her face was cracked with old tear streaks, but she was still breathing, slightly.

"Mom...." I whispered.

"Blair?" she coughed through a dry mouth, "You're... you're alive.."

"Mom..... what happened? I've searched everywhere for you.."

"I'm so sorry, honey. After the Velvet Queen attacked the camp, someone caught me and brought me here.."

"You've... been here for that long? Mom, I-"

"Sweetie, don't worry about me.. I'll be okay, but you need to get out of here."

"Mom, no.. I can't just leave you like this," my focus honed in at her dried intestines, "There has to be something I can do.. Tell me what to do, mom..."

Her graceful smile pierced through the agony, "Live, Blair. For both of us. For all of us. It's too late for me, but you and your friend have to go, now. I know you don't want to leave me, but you have to.. the world is counting on you."

"God dammit, mom! I don't care about the world! You are all I have left! I have to help you, I just have to!!"

"No, sweetie," she smiled," you have your friend, and you have our memories. I am so proud of... you. You're s-so s-s-strong and brave. So go on now... live for our memory. I love.. love.... love y-"

But before she could finish, she fell limp and lifeless, and the Deathborn faded in from behind her from a fiery silhouette.

"I see you finally found mommy," he mocked me, "just too bad I found her first, eh?"

He laughed as he tore her body from the cross with his teeth, swallowing her in lumps of dead flesh. My heart and mind froze in shock and panic.

"No more nonsense. It's time to end this game, little girl."

He raised his grand scythe back and swung so hard that the clouds themselves shifted. Fenrir pounced, knocking me out of the way, and caught the blade in his powerful jaws. They proceeded to tug back and forth, and Fenrir managed to crack off a piece of the blade's head.

"No dogs allowed!" said Deathborn.

His eyes had a green burn, and Fenrir was completely paralyzed in rigor within a conjured series of razor wire ropes that bound his legs and neck. My body swirled in blue and I drew my sword; I was ready to avenge my mother.

The battle between the Deathborn and I was on. I took a quick moment to observe the battle field. There wasn't a lot to work with, just a flat clearing with high walls, a few big boulders, and a cliff with about a thirty five hundred foot drop. He charged at me with one helluva force. The ground shook, his scythe shrieked as it drug across the ground, and I sprinted at him full force. No hesitation. The mountains echoed an ear bleeding ring when we collided. I leapt from the ground and my blade slid across his to the other side. I slashed across his face and he roared with anger, swinging his fist at me. The punch felt like getting hit by speeding train, and I could hear my ribs crack at the impact. The fight continued as a harsh barrage of swordplay and sorcery. We screamed loudly at the same time and our blades burned with a blue and green fire, and a great explosion combusted upon the massive encounter, knocking us both to opposite ends of the battle field. Everything was on fire, and I felt intense pain at my right hand. I looked down to see the worst case scenario; my hand burned to nothing but charred bone by the sheer heat of the explosion, and my sword broken in half by the collision.

The Deathborn approached slowly. His wicked green eyes glowing with the flames.

"No more family. No more Damien.. No more Mr. Death... No more Fenrir.... No more you...." he gawked coldly.

He made it ever apparent that I hadn't even been fighting him at full power, but he was at his limits now. He had become much larger and was now armed with six arms and six weapons. He was about to-

"Actually, it's SIR DEATH," my satchel wiggled, "you overgrown swamp donkey!"

There was a brief rattle of bones, and the remains of Sir Death hopped out, just the crispy skeleton of a rabbit. His flesh and fur were rapidly growing back before my very eyes.

"Sir Death... but how?" I asked.

"It's all thanks to you, my dear," he said, "Killing yourself just so you could bring my corpse into the Soul Chamber? Such a clever idea! Marvelous. Brilliant. Thanks to you, I was able to hitch a ride back. Now," he cracked his tiny knuckles, "I'll deal with this asshole; you have a queen to stab to death. So take your pup and get moving!"

I nodded my head and wrapped Fenrir's still paralyzed paws over my shoulders. As we walked away, Sir Death began to change. The little furry bunny's limbs extended out like long spider legs, and his soft hair was like black bloody skin, his teeth and claws grew sharp and slender like kris blades, and he was just as tall as the Deathborn. Yeah.. it's time to get our arses out of here.

The magic within me had numbed most of my pain and taken action on rejuvenating my injuries, but I was left with a stub at the end of my wrist and no weapon. Fenrir was heavy, and only having one hand to really hold him with was an extremely difficult task all on its own, not to mention how hard it is for a small girl to be carrying such a large body in the first place. Still, we proceeded onward. No matter how far we went, the battle raging behind us was of an epic, earth shaking tone. I could hear the clicks and clanks of blades and claws, the rumble of bodies being slammed, the roars of two creatures of death duking it out. Good luck, Sir Death.

My legs felt like hot jello, and my chest burned with a crushing weight. Fenrir's toes left blood streaks from being drug through the mountains for so long. I finally climbed us atop the next large mountain, though, and collapsed immediately. I was far too exhausted to continue at this rate. I laid back for a moment to rest up and took a short nap. After about an hour, I sat up and.. and there was this odd stone sticking up out of the ground. A huge, sword shaped stone. We were at Hero's Respite.

"The place where heroes come to pray for guidance," said Fenrir, with a groggy tone,

"Go on and pray, Blair. It won't be long now until it's time we face our destiny."

I approached the small shrine and closed my eyes. The world began to feel less and less lucid, and the strangest thoughts whispered through my head. For a moment, even, it felt like I was back home. It was an extraordinary sensation. Happy memories raced through my mind and when I opened my eyes, I found my hand to be completely restored and holding an unbroken sword. The Queen's castle wasn't far, merely an open field between here and there. I observed the giant rock for a bit and found a strange text with a slender hole in the center of it.

"Fenrir, what do you make if this? Can you read it?"

He looked at it for a bit and muttered to himself under his breath, "These characters are ancient, but I'm pretty positive it says:

'And behold when the day of righteousness has come, for whosoever holds the Cerulean Key shall wipe from the eyes of the world the tainted blood, and so unbind the wings of order.'

The blade pulsated in my hand like a heartbeat. I wonder... I raised my sword up towards the slot, and the two seemed to form a sort of magnetic connection. Small beams of blue light protruded from the stone and caressed the blade, taking it from my hand that it may hover about freely. Inching its way closer and closer, the sword fit perfectly into the stone.. just like a key into a lock. Someone began clapping from the other side of the stone..

"My, my. I'm impressed, to be honest," the Velvet Queen said as she walked to my side, "After all of my attempts to stop you, you've still managed to make it this far. You are a lot stronger than I thought."

"She's stronger than you can imagine," Fenrir shook with anger, "and it's you who is going to be stopped. For everyone you've ever hurt and for all of the evil you have done, this is where you end!"

"Blah, fucking blah," she replied, "Settle down, you imbecile. Or do I need to put you in your place, just like I did your dearly beloved?"

She turned her attention to me, "That is, after I dispose of this travesty."

Fenrir was overwhelmed with gargantuous anger and blindly charged between her and me. His claws tore slash marks into the mountain as he ran towards her. He pounced high into the air and cratered into her with all his might, but was caught by the throat midair, effortlessly, just before contact was made. Her sharp grip tightened around his esophagus as she pulled him close. I could feel his life fading. I rushed to my sword and struggled to pull it from the stone, but it was stuck completely. Wings composed of many different blades outstretched from the Velvet Queen's back in an unorganized fashion.

She drew them forth to Fenrir's sides, and kissed his soft lips, "I will always love you, dearest, and you will always be mine, and I yours.."

I saw a single tear form in her eye and fade away, just before tearing apart his body with her wings. Pieces of his corpse flung across the mountaintop.

Thunder clouds black as obsidian rolled in to cover the

entire sky. The world was cast in a dark shadow and blood rained heavily from the clouds. This is the moment I've been preparing for.

The thunder smashed hard and bolts of lightning tore into the world. The Velvet Queen peered into me like daggers with her crimson eyes, the blood from above dripping from those bladed wings, and the dark world raging behind her.

"We could have been allies, Blair. I offered you my help. I offered you a place by my side at the castle. You could have been my successor, Blair. But you cast my generosity back as if it were the waste of the world. And look what its cost you. You lost, your friends, your family... yourself. And now your existence itself will cease to be. You have NOTHING left. This is not the ending I wanted for you, but you've left me no choice."

Darkness swirled in front of her, and a long sword rose from the ground. She slowly approached me, dragging it behind her.

"You're right," I replied, "About me losing myself. I did lose everything, and for a time did forget who I was. And all the malicious actions you took to kill me, they only made me stronger. My mind.. my heart... all cast so deeply into the darkness. But you know what? I crawled my way back out. For this moment. Right here. With you. I am the hero of this story, and I will finish it. But you're wrong about something, too. I have one thing left.... killing you."

Her hand gently rest upon my cheek, "Poor child.. Poor, ignorant, foolish child."

Her arms raised swiftly with the sword above her head. My opportunity arose. This is my chance to end it. I pulled out the dagger Nero had given me, and plunged it deep into her heart. The Velvet Queen froze in time, choking on her own blood. The dagger fell apart and backed away.

Her sword rang as it hit the ground, and her body fell shortly after.

"You.. you bitch.. where did you g-"

And before she could finish, the hands of those she had damned reached up from the ground beneath her, violently ripping her into the Soul Chamber. Her scream faded with her life. All was quiet.

I stood there atop of Hero's Respite and watched as the silence and the clouds dispersed. And for once, with a glowing sunset, Deadland looked kind of... beautiful. All was calm and still, and th-

"I'm not done yet!!"

I turned frantically to the voice and felt the long black blade impale my stomach. It was the Velvet Queen. She was bound in chains and shackles, but had managed to tear a hole back into Deadland from the Soul Chamber. My feet leave the ground as she lifted me with the giant sword, and I felt more and more of my torso split as it slid across her razor sharp blade.

"I will have every soul, I will rule this world eternally, and I will make you suffer more with every life I take," her blades wings crossed over my throat, "Long live the Velvet Queen...."

"Long live the Cerulean Queen!" Fenrir's voice echoed from within the Soul Chamber, yanking back the Velvet Queen by her chains.

Her blade fell from me.

"Blair, your sword!" he shouted, struggling to hold her back.

I limped to the stone and pulled it out with ease.

Her eyes and mine interlocked, hers widening in terror.

"Off with her head," I said in one fell swoop, decapitating the Velvet Queen.

And just as with anyone else, once killed in the Soul

Chamber, she faded from existence, and would never be seen again.

Sir Death appeared beside me, kicking her screaming face down the mountainside.

"You've done it, Blair. You've saved them all."

The sounds of chains falling and locks unfastening reverberated throughout the world, and the souls of the residents of Deadland began traveling to their rightful places. The doors of Heaven and Hell had been freed, and order began to restore. The Soul Chamber and Oblivion had even opened up, and everyone inside poured out, save for the Velvet Queen, in a sort if deep sleep, to be sorted, as well. My mom and dad, Emma, Damien, and Fenrir and Selene all floating together, towards the Golden Gates of Heaven. They were asleep, with such peaceful smiles.

"Sir Death," I inquired, "I thought souls were erased if they died in the Soul Chamber; how did-"

He interrupted, "Because, dear Blair, you have brought miracles upon miracles.."

I took his word and watched the spectacle. And as the last of the souls passed on, I began to wonder of myself.

"Sir Death, what... what about me? How.. how do I get to Heaven? ....Sir Death?"

But he was gone, and in his place was a small blue crown. At long last, the worlds were at peace.

Funny to think it's only been six months, but here I am. The Cerulean Queen. Ruler of all of Deadland, with all the riches and all the land in the world, living in a grand castle, and with each person and creature serving me as their god. But, you know what... I don't want any of it. All I want is to go home, to Seattle, with my family and Damien, to our little three bedroom house.. But that's never going to happen.

Printed in the United States
By Bookmasters

Two Things I Know

God Saved Me for a Reason and
He's Not Finished with Me Yet

S. ROBERTS

authorHOUSE®

AuthorHouse™
1663 Liberty Drive
Bloomington, IN 47403
www.authorhouse.com
Phone: 1 (800) 839-8640

Published by AuthorHouse 03/21/2019

ISBN: 978-1-7283-0462-5 (sc)
ISBN: 978-1-7283-0461-8 (e)

Library of Congress Control Number: 2019903203

Print information available on the last page.

This book is printed on acid-free paper.

Contents

Part 5 Serving Jesus Christ

ACKNOWLEDGEMENTS

I would like to gratefully acknowledge a few of those who helped make this book a reality:

Thank you, Betty T, for speaking into my life many years ago, telling me that I should write a book. It took many years for me to respond but I heard you as you planted the seed.

Thank you to my daughter, Mardi, who encouraged me through the years to do this. She read and re-read this difficult story about my past and was able to suggest how to make it more personal and relatable.

Thank you, Anne and David, for your quick response to read the manuscript and provide the needed feedback. You encouraged me with your kind words that I'll never forget. I thank God for our friendship.

Thank you, Shannon, for motivating me to keep going. You saw me pause and nudged me with your encouraging words. You are a great friend and leader.

Thank you, Pastor Ron, for reading my manuscript and making the suggestions that you made. Thank you for being my Pastor, speaking into my life week after week, keeping me grounded in the Word.

Chaplain Don, thank you for encouraging me to press on to the end. You saw something in me that I didn't see and were a vital part to my most recent opportunity.

A huge thank you to my first responder, Chief Clabes. You were certainly an angel that night thirty six years ago when you were the first one on the scene. Thank you for your years of service to our community.

May God richly bless your lives and to Him be all the glory!

I'd like to thank Jesus Christ, my Lord and Savior.

Without His intervention, I would not be here today.

I dedicate this book to my family.

To my husband, Charlie, who loved me through
my full recovery and did not give up on me. You
believed in me when I didn't believe in myself.

To my girls who love me in spite of my imperfections and my
shortcomings as a mom. You are the family that I always hoped for.

To my Dad, Mom, Brother, and Sisters who loved me through
it all. We stuck together where some families fall apart.

I thank God for all of you and look forward
to spending eternity with you.

PREFACE

I publicly shared my testimony in 2006 when I spoke to a group of ladies at the church that I was attending. The following Sunday, my pastor's wife told me that I should write a book. Although I never thought I'd have what it would take to write a book, her words planted a seed in my heart.

Ten years later, I shared my story again with another group of women. Not long after, I wrote a paragraph, feeling that I had somewhat accomplished the goal. Once again, I pushed the idea to the back of my mind.

The following year, I attended a women's conference in Fort Worth, Texas. I picked up a copy of the presenter's daily pep talk and began to declare her words over my life. One of the daily declarations was, "I am fulfilling my life assignment down to the last detail." That began to stir something in my spirit. I started hearing myself say, "I am fulfilling my life assignment down to the last detail ... except my book."

At the beginning of this year, early one morning, I was going over in my head what I would do as I prepared to start writing. In my spirit, I heard the Lord say, "Write it down." I knew that it was time.

I left my full-time job to pursue writing as well as two other assignments given to me. God has given me a unique testimony of His saving grace. It is my desire to document the events that took place in my life, revealing what God can do in people's lives when they have decided that they have had enough of themselves and are ready to surrender to Him. Let everything that I include be to God's glory.

I pray that you will read this book with an open mind. I also pray that you will dare to believe that what God did for me, He can do for you and for your loved ones. He is no respecter of persons.

God bless you!

Susan

PART 1

Lost

April 1982

The first thing she saw when the gun went off was dust falling from the ceiling. With the light on in the hallway of her mobile home and the blast of the single gunshot, everything stopped except the falling of the dust. Being completely caught off guard, no one moved for a second or two trying to figure out what had just happened.

   She looked first at the ceiling and then at the floor expecting to see a hole blown through. Then she looked at her friend as he sat in the chair, head dropped back, eyes fixed. He was dead. He had killed himself.

CHAPTER 1

Childhood

Hi. I'm Susan. I initially wrote this book in the third person. I found it easier to share these events as if they were about someone else. Two trusted people in my life encouraged me to tell it as if it happened to me because it did happen to me. I am the person that this book is about—sort of. Really, the book is about the events that brought me to my knees. And it's about God, or Jesus Christ, and how He revealed Himself to me. It's about how He changed my life.

I'll start at the beginning and talk a bit about my childhood, although it wasn't at all dramatic or traumatizing. Actually, I came from a good home. It was very stable and predictable. I was the youngest of four kids, although we never lived together at the same time. By the time I was born, my oldest brother, Wayland, was headed to the navy. Next in line was Betty. Thirteen years after Betty came Deborah—or Deb as we call her. I remember my cousin Vickie sharing the story of what my mom said to Betty when she was pregnant with Deb. Mom asked, "What would you do if I told you I was pregnant?"

Betty said, "I'd yank my hair out."

My mom said, "Well, start yankin'!"

So thirteen-year-old Betty and sixteen-year-old Wayland had a baby sister on the way. They were all crazy about the new baby when she arrived. However, three years later, when my mom got pregnant with me, Wayland was in the navy and Betty was graduating high school and planning her wedding.

I believe that even though I was the baby of the family, Deb had got all of the attention. By the time I came along, I was just there. Now I can't prove that, but that's my theory! I'm sure there are others who would remember things differently! Deb tells me that she doesn't remember it being that way, but she has stories of her relationships with Wayland and Betty that I don't have. That's because they were gone when I got there. And besides, like I said, it's my story.

I loved my parents very much. My dad was an honest, hardworking man. I had a wonderful mother. It was my mom's job to take care of the home, the kids, and the school functions. Dad worked, first at Tinker Air Force Base and then in his single-car garage in the evenings. He had learned from a friend how to rebuild wrecked cars. This became his hobby. He was good at it, too. He would buy a totaled vehicle and tow it home with his pickup truck. Rarely did he ever hire a wrecker to bring it home. That would cost too much. However, he had a pretty good temper. My mom would try to keep peace, sometimes by keeping from him things we had done. I caught on to this real quick, and during my teenage years, I took full advantage of it.

The only fighting in the home was between Deb and me. It was the typical fighting among sisters that got us a spanking a time or two. However, there was no showing of affection—not between Mom and Dad and not between parents and children. I remember my dad kissing my mom on the cheek once at the urging of us kids, but he blushed, and they were clearly uncomfortable. I was never spontaneously hugged or kissed by my parents. I would kiss my dad on the cheek on my way to bed at night when I was very young. He returned the kiss on my cheek, but that was the extent of any affection. I was certainly never hugged tightly by either parent. I wasn't mistreated, just not shown any affection. I understand now that they were from a generation that believed showing affection, emotion, or sensitivity was a sign of weakness.

I remember how affectionate Betty and Jimmy, my brother-in-law, were with my nieces, LeAnn and Dana. They were just three and six years younger than me, so they were more like sisters in some ways. Their daddy would buy the small red boxes of candy on Valentine's Day for them. For Betty, he'd buy the big, beautiful box of candy.

Jimmy was a fireman. We would go with Betty to the fire station to see him when he was on duty. He'd walk out to the car in his uniform. He looked so handsome and always ended our visit by giving Betty and his girls a kiss when she started the car to leave. He'd wave goodbye to Deb and me. Jimmy was a good brother-in-law to us. My first memories as a child included him.

I just always wished my daddy was like that. I longed for someone to buy me something for Valentine's Day.

What I didn't understand, until I was much older, was that people show their love in different ways. My daddy showed his love, not by hugs and kisses but by going to work every day and by never having our utilities turned off because of nonpayment. He showed his love by never laying a hand on any of us, including my mom, except for that rare spanking for me or my sister. He never stayed out all night and never came home drunk. Not once.

Mom was the subservient wife, which was more common in those days. She made sure that three meals a day were provided. When my dad finished his food, he'd look toward the countertop, and Mom would go get the dessert. He didn't have to say anything. He just looked toward the dessert, and she'd get it.

My parents weren't social people. I wasn't raised in church, nor was I involved in any type of sport. My only opportunity to interact with others was at school and with extended family. My family would get together occasionally and have cookouts during the summer. We'd grill hamburgers and make homemade ice cream. We went to the lake, either an evening trip to Draper or a weekend trip to Lake Tenkiller. We went with aunts, uncles, and cousins. Betty and her family were there most, and we would have so much fun! I learned to water ski when I was a kid. All the kids learned to ski when we were around eight years old. We would wait our turn for the boat to come back, drop off a skier, circle back around, and get the next one. Going to the lake is something that my family still enjoys doing.

Occasionally, my brother would be there too. That was always a treat because I didn't get to see him often. After the navy, Wayland got married. I was too young to remember the wedding, but I knew my sister-in-law and remember when they had their son. Wayland named his son after our dad, whose name was James. They called the baby Jay. Not long after Jay was born, Wayland and Jay's mom divorced. She and Jay moved to Oregon.

I had a couple of neighborhood friends. However, I was envious of my friends when they made other friends or did something with others because that wasn't easy for me to do. I was jealous of those who were outgoing and connected with others easily, especially girls. As I got older, it became easier to be friends with boys than with girls. I didn't have to compete, and the boys liked me more than girls did. The difficulty connecting with more than one or two girls at a time would remain until adulthood. There was always that sense of jealousy or competition.

All through elementary school, I was at the head of the class. My teachers liked me. I was quiet. I was a great student and made straight As. Some of my teachers would have me stay in during recess and help with the bulletin boards. Other kids were jealous and wondered why I got to stay in and help. This wasn't the case in middle school and certainly was not the case in high school. By then, I had turned inward.

I wanted to disappear.

CHAPTER 2

Adolescence

I started using drugs as a teenager. I was smoking pot by the time I was fourteen. I wasn't scared to try it. Actually, I looked forward to the opportunity. Something about me was unhappy. I was unhappy with myself—my personality, and my looks. I wanted to be talkative and happy-go-lucky, but instead I was quiet and shy. And I was tall! Too tall! I was always the tallest girl in the class all through school, even in elementary school. I didn't mind it so much until I became a teen, and all of the girls around me started filling out. I just seemed to grow taller. And I was thin or skinny. I hated being thin. People would call you "skinny," which seemed weird because they wouldn't call you fat—not to your face anyway! I remember overhearing some girls talk one time. One said, "She's pretty, but I wouldn't want to be that skinny." Well, neither did I! I couldn't help being thin. Or they would ask me, "Girl, why are you so skinny?" I thought, *Well, why are you so _____?* Fill in the blank. I would never ask a person something like that!

Because I was so quiet and such an introvert, it was never suspected that I would be the instigator when something happened. One day in middle school, I wrote my friend's initials in nail polish on the table in home economics class. Of course, I wouldn't write my *own* initials. I wrote my best friend's! Needless to say, I wasn't a very good friend. The teacher saw it and accused my friend. She denied it but didn't tell on me. The teacher went around the table and said to every girl, "Did you do it?" Then to the next, "Did you do it?" She went to every girl at the table, and they all said no, but still, no one told who it really was. When she got to me she said, "I know you didn't do it." Boom! I got away with it. This seemed to be the case time and time again. Rarely did I have to face consequences.

One year, some of my friends and I went to the state fair. Inside one of the buildings, I slipped a pair of earrings that were on display into my smock pocket. The man behind the counter, who seemed to have eyes in the back of his head, took me by the arm and said, "Come on, we're going to see the police." The other girls walked out of the building afraid of what was going to happen. I begged the man to let me go. He did! Whew! That was close, but I did learn, and I never did that again!

I made it through middle school and then to high school progressing in my defiant behavior and drug use. I was open to other drugs as well, which is often the problem with recreational drug use. When you're open to one type, then why not another?

I skipped school on a regular basis. Still trying to keep these things from my dad, my mom would call in for me the next day and make an excuse for my absence. This would sometimes get tricky when the school called my home and my dad, who was retired by then, was still sitting at the breakfast table. I just about wore my mother out with my behavior. At that time, however, I wasn't concerned about my mother. I was only concerned about myself.

I got high every day at school. This was no exaggeration. I would see Deb in the hallway after lunch. Deb could always tell by my eyes that I was high and would give me "the look." I was known among my peers as someone who always had drugs. This pattern and lifestyle was what shaped my teenage and high school years.

I was known as "Debbie's little sister." Some kids may have wanted their own identity rather than be known as someone's little sister, but not me. Deb was pretty and was popular with girls, as well as boys, so I liked being called that. Besides, having a big sister meant you got to ride in cars and go places with the older kids.

Not too long after Deb graduated from high school, she moved out of the house following a little spat with our parents about curfew. Deb left and never moved back in. I had always tagged along with Deb when we were younger, but this time, I didn't get to go. I took this hard, but no one seemed to notice, or at least it was never mentioned.

CHAPTER 3

Young Adult

When I graduated from high school, I was working but I fully believed that life was a party, and I was living it to the fullest! I couldn't wait to move out of my parent's home, and I found a friend to share an apartment with. My friend was everything that I was not. She was funny and was very uninhibited, which gave me permission to loosen up! We loved to drink and smoke pot together. The party was at our house! My roommate had a lot of friends, so we were having the time of our lives!

I had a good job and managed my money well. We only kept the lease on the apartment for six months. After that, my dad helped me buy a trailer house that I would live in alone for the next six years. I liked living alone. I still saw my former roommate on a regular basis, but we did better not living together. However, the party was still at my house!

I worked for a small utility supply company when I moved into the trailer. I was very efficient at my job, and my boss liked me. It was a one-girl office, and we would all occasionally go out for lunch and have drinks. After just over three years there, my boss and one of the salesmen made the decision to start their own company just like the one for which we were working. The men wanted me to go with them and help them with the start-up of their new company. I loved working for these guys and didn't want to be left out so, of course I would go!

Unfortunately, the change was not good for me. It was the first time that I made a change of jobs, and I felt completely inadequate. At the former company, the bookkeeping had been done by our headquarters, but this time, they wanted me to do the books. I had never had any real training for that. It was a much farther drive from my home. It was located across town when the other place was five minutes away. I had gone from something so familiar to something that I didn't like at all. I felt very inadequate, and things quickly began to deteriorate. Rather than admitting to and facing the fact that I had made a mistake, I began to use more and more drugs as a way of escape. It was the only way that I knew how to cope. Certainly, my head wasn't clear enough to learn bookkeeping.

During this time, some pills called Quaaludes were going around. This was my new choice drug because they made me loosen up. I felt great when I was on these pills, and I really didn't care about anything or anybody. I remember a night being high on Quaaludes, but it was getting late, and I needed to go to sleep so I could be at work the next morning. I didn't want to sleep, though, because I was enjoying the way I felt. Finally, I went to bed, but I woke up the morning as straight as a string. I was out of pills and depressed.

At work, customers, who were very confident of my past ability, were talking about how I didn't sound like I used to. My speech was slurred, and I was moody, they said. The owners started interviewing someone to take my place, apparently thinking that I was too out of it to notice. Six months into the new business, they let me go. This was a huge blow to my self-esteem at age twenty-two.

I was able to draw unemployment benefits, but my former bosses were eager for me to find another job. I applied for an open position at an oil company, and with their recommendations, I got the job. However, the next company did not get the efficient, organized worker that I once was. Instead, they got a girl that was well on her way to becoming a drug addict.

CHAPTER 4

Darkness

During the break between the two jobs, things really went downhill. A man that I had known for some time introduced me to meth. Through this man, I met a couple with whom I became close friends. The husband was into some dark criminal activity. He talked about the "family" although he never said who they were or what they did. He did say things like, "You don't want to know." He had a riddle about keeping a secret. I don't remember the words except that the expression was something like, "If he couldn't keep a secret, how could he expect me to be so bold?"

I was working at my new job, but because I was now using meth, my physical and mental health began to decline. Weight was falling off of me. I got sick with pneumonia and was off work for a week. I was late most days or didn't come in at all. This job, somehow, lasted six months but not because they didn't try. My new boss even took me to talk to his pastor. Soon, they had no choice but to let me go. This would be job number two that I lost due to drug abuse.

April 1982

Shortly after losing my second job, my new guy friend and some of his friends were at my house and had been for several days. There were drugs and guns, which was normal for these folks. The men would leave for several hours at a time. My friend and three other men returned to my house one afternoon. Another man had called to talk to him. He was on the phone, and the others were waiting for him to finish.

I was standing in the kitchen, about fifteen or twenty feet in front of him, when I heard a gunshot. It startled all of us, and I looked up from what I was doing. I remember the hall light being on, and the first thing I saw was dust falling from the ceiling because of the blast inside of the small trailer house. I looked up at the ceiling and then down at the floor expecting to see a hole blown through it, but I didn't see anything. I looked at my friend, who was sitting in the chair with his head dropped back and eyes fixed. He had killed himself. I was hysterical. Suddenly, there was a lot of movement inside as people starting gathering their belongings. I walked past his body to the back of the trailer to get on the other phone to tell the person that he was talking to what had happened. While I was out of the room, two of the three men left. When I returned, the gun was gone.

The remaining man promised to go and see if he could find the men and the gun and asked me to wait to call the police. I was left at home alone with my friend, who was now dead. After a while, I knew they weren't coming back, so I called the police. At first I tried to make up a story with fake names, but finally I told them the truth. They took me to the police station as a material witness and kept me there from about 6:00 p.m. until 2:00 a.m. With no weapon, it was hard to rule suicide, and because of what he was involved in, they wanted to rule it a homicide. However, because of the position of the body, the furniture, etc., it was finally ruled a suicide. Not only did he lose his life that night; I lost the person who would protect me and tell me to watch out for this one or that one.

I had cooperated with the police and feared that I may have said too much. I wished I could go back and start all over. Some people encouraged me and said that I had handled things well. Others asked me why I told the police this or that. I began to sense evil and started to become afraid.

There was a group of people interested in talking to me. They invited me to come out to a house on Memorial Day weekend. They promised that we would go to Turner Falls, which was somewhere that I had always wanted to go but had never been. On that day, however, it was raining, so we didn't go to Turner Falls.

The man that lived there asked me about our friend that had died. "What happened that day?" he asked. I recounted the events of the day and explained that he had killed himself. He asked me if the friend had told me about some of the things that he had done. I told him that I knew that he had done some bad things but that I cared for him anyway. So I sat and watched the rain and cried as I grieved the loss of my friend.

Sometime after that, a trailer house was moved in next door to my trailer. Prior to that, the lot was empty. My new neighbor was friendly enough. He asked me to let the worker from the telephone company into his house while he was at work one day. The worker happened to be a guy that I had graduated high school with, and I told him about what had happened the month before at my house. People—especially my family—warned me to be careful. As expected, they were very concerned!

Police Probe Man's Death

Midwest City police were seeking information Friday to determine whether a shooting that left one man dead is a murder or suicide.

"We're kind of in a quandary about it until we find out more information," one detective said of the Thursday night shooting that killed ████ 39. Police said he had a rural route address in Oklahoma City.

████ was dead at the scene of a single gunshot wound to the head, police spokesman Ed Forman said. No weapon has been recovered.

"It is possibly a homicide, although there is a good possibility it could be a suicide," he said.

Police said ████ and two other men were visiting Susan Roberts at her mobile home.

Summer 1982

The newest group of people had a very pure and powerful source of meth. One night, back at that house, we were all using, and I knew as soon as the drug had hit my system that I had gotten too much! I was very high—more so than I had ever been. The best way to describe what happened was that within this high was another high, and it was drawing me to it. It was very appealing. I somehow recognized this "high" as death. It scared me so bad that in my spirit, I said, "Oh, God, please don't let me die!" Immediately, I stopped being drawn and started coming back, moving back away from the thing that had been drawing me.

Something happened that night. I believe that even though I didn't know Him, I cried out to God, and He heard me. He not only stopped me from dying, He entered my situation, as bad as it was. I believe that God placed a hedge of protection around me. In the days and weeks ahead, I was going to need it!

August 1982

One evening around nine o'clock or so, I had gone to the grocery store and had bought a couple of bags of groceries for myself. When I got back to my house, because I was afraid of being outside alone, I had walked to the passenger side of my car and picked up both bags. I walked up the steps to the front door of my trailer house. I propped the screen door on my shoulder and was unlocking the front door when I heard a slight sound behind me. Just then, something struck me hard in the lower back. It had a lot of force behind it, but I had no idea what it could have been. As I turned to look behind me, the shaft of an arrow caught on the door and fell to my feet. At that point, I realized that I had been shot with an arrow. I dropped the groceries and fell to my knees, screaming and looking into the darkened window of the trailer next door. I was thinking that my neighbor next door would help me! He had been hanging around trying to be my friend. But I realized that all of his lights were off, so apparently he wasn't home. I felt that I needed to get inside the trailer where I'd be safe. I crawled inside and called the police, who called an ambulance for me. I could feel a hole in my lower back the size of my middle finger.

I had been fairly calm until the ambulance attendants got there. They seemed so serious that it freaked me out. My blood pressure had dropped so low that they thought they were going to lose me. I felt as though I would pass out! They put some type of pants on my lower body that pumped up like a blood pressure sleeve. Later someone told me it was a type of tourniquet, as they were trying to keep the blood circulating to my vital organs.

By the time they got me out of the trailer and to the ambulance, a crowd of onlookers had gathered. My neighbor's light was on now. The ambulance drivers took me to Midwest City Hospital where, once inside, the police asked me if I knew of anyone that was trying to kill me. I told them no and was a little surprised that they thought someone was really trying to kill me. I was terribly naive.

I was transferred to Saint Anthony's hospital that same night. They were concerned about removing the tip of the arrow because it was lodged in my back, just left of my spine—two centimeters, to be exact.

They removed it the next day manually, by just pulling it out the same way it went in. It was extremely painful. I was in the hospital for a week. When I was discharged my parents wanted me to go straight to rehab, but I refused. I was going to do this on my own. I left there with no follow-up instructions and nothing for pain. My parents' next-door neighbor, a retired RN, removed the stitches from my back two weeks later.

Meanwhile, the police made an arrest. Only by asking me questions such as was I wearing shoes, where was I standing when I was struck, which way did I turn, etc., it was determined that the arrow had to have come from the window of the trailer house next door. They arrested the next-door neighbor and accused him of being inside of his trailer with the lights off, window open, and screen removed when he shot me. He was bound over for trial for shooting with intent to kill.

On the day of the trial, while I was waiting in the witness room, I was approached by a nicely dressed young lady and was told to go home, as there weren't enough judges to hear all of the cases. I was told to call back the next day for further instructions. However, when I called the courthouse the next day, I was told that the charges had been dismissed against the man. They were having his trial when I was told to go home, and since I didn't "show up" as a witness, the charges against him were dropped.

I received threatening phone calls telling me "there will be no more charges filed." I was still clueless as to whom and what I was dealing with. The trailer next door was moved out. The park owner asked me to move as well because the neighbors were scared. He talked to me about Jesus, and I cried. He was the first person that I can remember who talked to me about my need for the Lord.

My trailer house was moved out of that park and into another just a few miles away. It wouldn't be long until people knew where I was and would start coming around again.

ST. ANTHONY HOSPITAL
OKLAHOMA CITY

HISTORY & PHYSICAL
OA-133-B

ROBERTS, SUSIE
82-113635-8

Adm. 8-6-82

ROGER JANITZ, D.D.S.,RES.
B. J. RUTLEDGE, M.D.

This is a 23-year-old white female who was admitted with a complaint of being shot in the back with an arrow. She was walking into the front door of her trailer home, when she felt something stick her in the back. When she turned around, she broke off the shaft of what appears to be the hub. She was initially seen in Midwest City E.R. where she was stable and moving her lower extremities. She had complaint of faint numbness in her left foot. She had no bowel or bladder complaints. Foley was inserted, and urine was noted to be clear. She was then transferred to St. Anthony Hospital E.R. for evaluation and treatment.

Her vital signs are normal. BP 130/70, T 98.2, P 68, R 16.

PHYSICAL EXAMINATION:
Well-developed, well-nourished, 23-year-old white female in moderate distress lying supine on the backboard. She was oriented times three. She had complaint of pain and tightness in the back, and moving all fours.
HEENT: Head is normocephalic. Pupils are equal, round and reactive to light. EOMs are intact. Fundi flat, TMs are intact bilaterally. Nose is patent. Throat clear.
NECK: Full range of motion.
CHEST: Heart revealed regular rate and rhythm without murmur. Chest clear to auscultation and percussion.
ABDOMEN: Muscular, supple, without tenderness. Normal active bowel sounds.
GENITALIA: Normal female. Pelvic not done. Foley in place, with clear urine.
RECTAL: Examination was not done.
EXTREMITIES: Reflexes were equal and symmetrical in both lower and upper extremities. Upper extremities grips were equal. Muscles were 5/5 and there was no sensory deficit to pinprick. In lower extremities, she moved both legs. Muscles are 5/5 bilaterally. Sensation is intact to pinprick with negative Babinski's.
BACK: 1" laceration just to the left of the midline with a blood-soaked sponge stuffed in the wound. It was not removed. The area was cleaned with alcohol sponges and sterile 4x4s were placed and taped. Hemostasis was intact.

In the E.R., we started 1 gram of Mandol IV and D5 with ½ normal Saline at TKO rate. Lumbar films revealed 4x4x5 razor point arrow tip approximately 2½ to 3" in length, lodged 2 cm. left of the midline between the lamina of L3-4, possibly intradural or into the superior aspect of L4 body.

IMPRESSION:
Arrow tip in lumbar spine, L3-4 level, left.

PLAN:
Bedrest and observation and IV fluids and antibiotics. CAT scan in the a.m., L3-4, to check position of arrow tip before removal.
BJR:dkg
d/t 8-6-82 Line 5
dictated by Roger Janitz, D.D.S.,RES.
                                        B. J. RUTLEDGE, M.D.

Woman shot with arrow

MIDWEST CITY — A woman shot in the lower back with a hunting arrow Thursday night is in good condition at St. Anthony Hospital, while charges are being sought against the man suspected of shooting her.

Susan W. Roberts, 23, a resident of the Hill Top Trailer Park, was hit with the arrow shortly after 10 p.m., police Maj. James Cox reported. After interviewing area residents and checking the flight of the arrow, police said they are requesting the district attorney's office file charges of assault and battery with the intent to kill against _____, 29, also a resident of the trailer park.

Arrow Hits Woman in Back

A Midwest City woman remained hospitalized Friday night in stable condition after a hunting arrow pierced her back as she tried to unlock the door of her mobile home.

Susan Roberts, 23, of 9800 NE 21, was attempting to enter her trailer about 10:30 p.m. Thursday when she was struck by the arrow in her lower back, authorities said.

Medical personnel had to remove the four-speared point manually, according to Ray Elliott, assistant Oklahoma County district attorney.

_____, 29, was charged Friday with assault with a deadly weapon with intent to kill in the incident. He was booked into the Oklahoma County Jail on $15,000 bond.

Midwest City police arrested _____, whose mobile home stands about 15 feet from Roberts', at the scene.

Fall 1982

Over the next few weeks and months, I realized that being shot with the arrow wasn't a random act of violence but an attempted murder. Needless to say, I was very afraid. I also became so paranoid that I suspected that everyone was trying to kill me. I would have to reason with myself that my family wasn't involved. I just about lost it.

My brother was a long-haul truck driver and had been for years. He invited me to go on the road with him, which got me out of town for a few days. I went and enjoyed this time on the road with Wayland. He would let me have the sleeper one night, and then the next night I had to sleep in the seat while he got the sleeper so that he could get some rest. We drove from Oklahoma City to New Jersey and then back. He knew people all across the country at truck stops, as he was a regular customer. I cherished that time because I didn't always have a lot of time with my brother. We talked about everything.

I stayed at my parents' home for a while, too scared to go back to the trailer alone. When I finally did go home, I realized that to change my luck, I'd have to change my lifestyle.

PART 2

Restoration

CHAPTER 5

Salvation

I had a friend from high school stop by to see me every now and then. He had become a Christian. He was going to church regularly and invited me to go with him, and I finally went. He was working for a company and told me that they might be hiring. I applied there, and with his recommendation, I got the job. I worked the evening shift at a warehouse stocking car parts. I came home each night after midnight.

My friend had told me about Jesus and salvation. It was something that he had received. Intrigued, I asked what salvation felt like. He explained that when he asked Jesus to come into his heart, it felt like a load was lifted off of his shoulders. So one night, in my house when I was alone, I got on my knees and asked Jesus to forgive me of my sins and to come into my heart.

> Therefore, if anyone is in Christ, he is a new creation; old things have passed away; behold, all things have become new. (2 Corinthians 5:17 NKJV)

He was right. I felt the weight lift off of my shoulders! Although I was not instantly delivered from my addiction to meth, I did want to get clean. I did not want to continue living the way that I had been.

During this time, I came across a small red booklet. I was so moved by the words that I wrote some of them down before giving it back to its owner. The booklet, *From One of the Survivors*, said, "Why would anyone continue to do something that promised so much pain, heartache and destruction? Why, Satan's no fool! He's been around for a long, long time." Many years later, I remember those words. I don't know the name of the writer, nor do I remember who loaned the booklet to me, but the message is still burned into my memory.

As a matter of fact, I was reading and soaking up anything that was inspiring change. I had somehow heard of a Bible that was written in everyday language. I went to a local Christian bookstore and asked the clerk about it. She knew just what I was looking for; the *New International Version*. So, I bought myself a Bible! The Word of God became my source! I was so hungry for something pure that I would read the Bible, holding it in one hand and a dictionary in the other. I wanted to understand every word that I was reading. It was bringing life back into my lifeless body. It was restoring my soul and renewing my mind.

I remember lying on my bed one night, reading my Bible. I paused, laid the book down on my lap, and thought to myself, *I wonder if this is real?* Just then, waves of what felt like electricity started at the top of my head and went all the way down to my feet. It went through my body about four times. Just waves of the presence of the Lord flowing through my body. *This is real!* I thought.

There was another time that I read something about witnessing for the Lord, which meant telling people about Jesus. This was all so new to me that I remember thinking that I couldn't imagine myself doing that!

As I mentioned before, I wasn't immediately delivered from my addictions. I went to work many days at the warehouse under the influence. I was malnourished, and working at the warehouse was hard work. It wasn't something that I could physically keep up with while not eating or sleeping. Eventually, I would work all week and use only on the weekend. Then a weekend would go by that I didn't use. The next weekend, I would use it again. I got frustrated with myself because I felt like I took two steps forward and one step back. However, I was moving, and I was moving in the right direction. It was a process, and

I've told people since then that I had to "walk it out." It took a full year to regain my health, my confidence, and my status as a good employee.

My old "friends" came around, but their visits became less often. They knew that I didn't trust them, so it became risky for them to come to my house. However, during this time, I know that I was followed, and I'm sure that my house was bugged. I believe that people were moved into one of the rentals in the new trailer park. Someone had been in my house once when I ran to my parents' house for lunch. I came back quicker than I normally did, and things were left out of place. They knew my routine.

CHAPTER 6

Transition

The Lord is my Shepherd
I shall not want. He maketh me to lie down in green pastures
He leadeth me beside the still waters. He restoreth my soul. He
leadeth me in the path of righteousness for his name's sake. Yea,
though I walk through the valley of the shadow of death, I will
fear no evil for thou art with me. Thy rod and thy staff, they
comfort me. Thou preparest a table before me in the presence of
mine enemies, thou anointest my head with oil, my cup runneth
over. Surely goodness and mercy shall follow me all the days
of my life and I will dwell in the house of the Lord forever!

I began to memorize scripture. The first thing I memorized was the
Twenty-Third Psalm. Somehow, it was familiar from childhood.

I would recite those verses when afraid or outside alone. "I will fear
no evil for thou art with me." I was often afraid coming in alone after
midnight. Occasionally, there would be a rabbit near the back of my
trailer that I could see when I pulled into my driveway. I always felt
safe when the rabbit was there because I knew he wouldn't be there
if someone was hiding behind my trailer. I really felt that this was
something that God did for me. It was a reminder that He was with
me and that I was not alone.

There was a night that I came home and the door to my water heater had come open and was blowing open and closed in the strong wind. I walked back to the end of the trailer to latch it back but feared that it was a setup. These stories may sound crazy but this was my thinking at that time. Coming in after dark alone, knowing that someone had wanted me dead, was very scary. It was hard for me to shake the fear. If someone ran toward me, even during daylight, or if a car seemed to approach me in a parking lot, I would think in the back of my mind, *Is this it?*

I finally told one guy from this group that I didn't know anything that would get any of them into trouble. My friend who killed himself at my house made sure that he didn't tell me anything. He would say, "You don't want to know!" Eventually, I never saw any of them again. I felt that the Lord delivered me from the hand of my enemies.

I worked evenings at the warehouse for a full year when they offered me a day position. I had promised myself that I wouldn't work another summer in that hot warehouse, so I declined their offer and used the daytime to look for a better job. I was ready to move into something that I enjoyed more. By this time, I was rarely using.

Even though I had become a Christian and my life was slowly transitioning, I have to say that this was one of the most difficult times in my life. I had traded all of my old friends in for the new ones—the meth users. When I left the users, my life was void of friends because my old friends had moved on. I felt extremely alone. Silly as it sounds, I remember thinking about the old Hank Williams Sr., song "I'm So Lonesome, I Could Cry." I had never felt so alone.

I read a chapter in Kahlil Gibrans's book *The Forerunner.* In it there is a parable called "Said a Snow White Sheet of Paper." The parable is about a snow white piece of paper that vows to never let darkness (ink) touch it. All the writing instruments heard her, so they never approached her. So the snow white piece of paper stayed pure and chaste forever: "pure and chaste—and empty." That's how I felt during this time. Empty. I'll never forget how I identified with that blank sheet of paper.

Everything had been stripped away. This is where someone else may have gone back to the drugs. My situation was different, and there was no going back. I had no choice but to keep moving forward.

I know now that God had a purpose for that.

CHAPTER 7

Answered Prayer

This is the confidence we have in approaching God: that
if we ask anything according to His will, He hears us.

—1 John 5:14 NIV

God was doing a work in me. I was learning to trust Him more and
more. I recognized that He was answering my prayers as He was building
a relationship with me.

I started applying for jobs at different companies. Finally, after
several rejections, I got an offer working for the accounts payable
department at the headquarters of one of the nationwide retail stores. I
only used the drug once while working there. I remember feeling like
everyone was staring at me. I never used it again after that. That was a
characteristic that I no longer wanted associated with me.

Thankfully, I recognized God's faithfulness to me during this time
as I continued seeking Him. I asked in faith that He would send me
a mate. I prayed specifically for someone with whom I could worship
Him. God was faithful to answer that prayer. I learned that when you
pray a prayer that honors God, He'll answer your prayer and give you
the desires of your heart. He also knew that I needed someone.

God sent me my mate—my soul mate and my stabilizer. I met my husband-to-be that summer. Charlie was a man grieving the loss of his twenty-eight-year-old wife. She died from cancer, leaving him with two little girls, Annie and Lora. We started dating, and he asked me to marry him on the first Valentine's Day that we were together. We married that summer.

It wasn't long after that when I found out I was expecting a baby. The place where I worked showered me with gifts first for the wedding, and then a few months later, they showered me again for the baby. We chose not to know the gender until the baby was born. It was a girl! My husband was clearly outnumbered now, with three girls and a wife! Even our German shepherd dog was a girl!

Once again, being concerned with what people thought about me was helpful for me to stop another bad habit. I felt like people were looking at me and judging me while I was pregnant and smoking. I remember my OBGYN suggested that I do myself a favor and stop smoking. So I did. Actually, we did. At the beginning of my third trimester, Charlie and I both quit smoking cigarettes. It was hard to do, but we did it, and it was worth the effort. Nowadays, they have a lot of help for people trying to quit. Back then, it was cold turkey!

PART 3

Setback

CHAPTER 8

Addiction Revisited

Be alert and of sober mind. Your enemy the devil prowls
around like a roaring lion looking for someone to devour.

—1 Peter 5:8 NIV

I'd like to say that it was easy and that I was a wonderful wife and
mother. I wish I could say, "And they all lived happily ever after. The
end." Actually, it was the opposite! Or, I was the opposite. Being a wife,
and especially being a mom, was hard for me. The stress, so quickly after
my "ordeal," took its toll on me. I had not processed the things that I
had been through in the past. I wasn't nearly as patient and as nurturing
as I should have been with the girls. I had a lot of pity parties, and, quite
truthfully, I was just mean at times. I was depressed and angry. I made
mountains out of mole hills. I had headaches, and I slept a lot in my
spare time. I just wanted to pull the covers up over my head in hopes
that it would all go away.

Eventually, I was given a prescription for barbiturates to help with
the headaches. However, as strange as it seemed, I noticed that I enjoyed
things more when I took the pills! Little things like being at home all
day with the kids or going to the mall were more fun when taking the
meds. It wasn't long before I was taking them every day whether I had

a headache or not. I found myself self-medicating. It wasn't even that I was getting high from the drugs. I never took more than one at a time, but I was abusing them and not taking them as prescribed. I used them as a preventative plus they helped me sleep. They made me "feel better." Those old behaviors had resurfaced.

After about a year of this, I admitted to myself that I had a problem. I was so disappointed in myself. I felt like I had been blindsided. After all that I had been through, how did I end up here again? How could I be so stupid?

During this time, I worked for a group of psychologists, and a patient had brought in a box full of self help books. I was allowed to pick through the books and take some home. One of the books was titled *Willpower's Not Enough*, written by Arnold Washton, PhD, and Donna Boundy, MSW. It was a book about recovering from addictions of every kind. I started reading about the many types of behaviors and learned some things from this book about myself and my addictive behavior. One thing that stood out in this book was, "If you're trying to control something, you've already got a problem." That was revolutionary to me.

I asked a counselor that I was seeing during this time if what I heard years before was true: once an addict, always an addict? Her explanation was, "once an addict, always addictive."—meaning the potential was there, but a person was clearly not always doomed to be a drug addict. It was with her assistance that I got the help that I needed. I was placed on an antidepressant and was prescribed medication for headaches that was not habit forming. This made a huge difference in my life. The antidepressant took the edge off and helped me to not dwell on the negative. It helped me to not make such a big deal out of things. Although it was hard to admit that I needed medication, it had become a quality of life issue. I was a sound Christian but just had not corrected all of my thinking. Those deep-rooted behaviors had not yet been dealt with.

It was during this time that I recognized some things about substance abuse and chemical dependency. The thought will come into your mind. And, back to the booklet that I came across when I was dealing with the hard drugs, which said, "Why, Satan's no fool.

He's been around for a long, long time." He knows our weaknesses. He knows *your* weaknesses. He'll try one thing, and if that doesn't work, he'll circle back around with something else. He'll bring another temptation packaged to look different. Sometimes the temptations are back to back. Sometimes, it's with that second one that you recognize his voice and you call him out. "I recognize you, Satan. You have no authority here!"

PART 4

Don't Give Up

CHAPTER 9

A Work in Progress

If we confess our sins, he is faithful and just to forgive us
our sins, and to cleanse us from all unrighteousness.

—1 John 1:9 KJV

I'm still somewhat surprised that over thirty years later, the thoughts still cross my mind. The difference is that I no longer go there. I've learned to recognize the source, call it out, and not give in to the temptations that present themselves. However, I continue to be a work in progress in many areas of my life. I'm not perfect, and I never will be while on this earth. I have processed the things of the past and know that it's not about "feeling better." Feelings are not how we are to live our lives. Feelings are great as long as you aren't led by them. Otherwise, why not live by the motto "if it feels good, do it"? That is about as destructive as it gets.

Listening to our pastor preach one Wednesday night, he talked about our need to have a vision for our lives. I realized that was what I had back in the early eighties. I had a vision for my life: for more than what I was living at that time. Rather than a poverty level, drug-laden life, I wanted more. God had put something in me to want more out of life than that. Proverbs 29:18 says, "Where there is no vision the people perish." Had I not wanted more—had a greater vision for my life than what I was living—I would have perished.

But I also realized that something more was not just going to fall on me. Like salvation, you have to do something about it. Invite Jesus into your situation, whatever it might be. Be it substance abuse, marital issues, or financial or spiritual matters, you can call on the Lord, and He will hear you. He won't fix it for you but, if you let Him, He'll help you as you walk it out. In his book *Draw the Circle: The 40 Day Prayer Challenge*, Mark Batterson says that we have to "pray like it depends on God but work like it depends on us." That's putting our faith into action. The Bible says in James 2:17: "in the same way, faith by itself, if it is not accompanied by action, is dead." In other words, faith without works is dead.

Can you really change? What about your loved ones? What about your child that seems determined to self-destruct? The answer is yes. God can change things and people. We can't, but He can. There's hope for your marriage that seems beyond repair. You can recover financially if you'll start doing things differently. Learn all that you can and do all that you can while you're waiting for your breakthrough. As long as we are alive, there is hope. No matter what the situation is, there is hope.

CHAPTER 10

Don't Give Up on Yourself

For I am convinced that neither death nor life, neither angels nor demons, neither the present nor the future, nor any powers, neither height nor depth, nor anything else in all creation, will be able to separate us from the love of God that is in Christ Jesus our Lord.

—Romans 8:38–39 NIV

Oftentimes, we are our own worst enemy. We beat ourselves up when we say something wrong. We sabotage our lives, relationships, and opportunities because we are afraid of failure, rejection, and even at times, we fear success! Fear runs rampant in our minds if we don't take those thoughts captive. You can bet that if the enemy is involved, it's a lie. We have to go to the Word of God to find the truth on every matter, and the truth sets us free! Hebrews 4:12 says, "For the word of God is alive and active. Sharper than any double-edged sword, it penetrates even to dividing soul and spirit, joints and marrow; it judges the thoughts and attitudes of the heart."

We have to get over our victim mentality and realize that no matter what's been done to you or who did it, it's up to you to take one step at a time and pull yourself up out of that. Declaring yourself a victim and blaming someone else for your life's problems keeps you in the bondage that you are in.

Some of you truly are innocent victims, and I don't minimize that. I was not. I got myself into the mess that I was in. But even if you truly are a victim of someone else's bad behavior, it's still up to you to pull yourself up out of that mind-set. Ask God for His help. It may be that you need the help of a physician or counselor. There's nothing wrong with that. We all need someone to talk to. Sometimes we may need medication to help us get on track as we walk it out. God uses people. He uses professionals as well. We aren't meant to live our lives alone. We need each other. As you talk to godly people, be sure to talk to God as well. He will guide you to the right scripture as you walk it out. Return to the Word, time after time, declaring the truth about who you are.

It was important to me that my parents didn't give up on me. I'd say to my dad, "Just don't give up on me!" He would admit that sometimes that was hard to do. He was by my side during those trying times, and I know I was responsible for a lot of his sleepless nights. He went to the police station after I had been shot, telling them that "we aren't just going to sweep this under the rug." He went to court with me on more than one occasion.

My mom would sit with me when I was afraid. She would cook a full meal at lunchtime for my dad and would expect me to come and eat too, making sure that I ate a decent meal before going to work at the warehouse.

Many years after my conversion, I was blessed to pray the prayer of salvation with both Mom and Dad before they passed away. God was faithful to me again, by answering my prayer for their salvation.

If you believe that God has forgiven you, be willing to forgive yourself. You have to love yourself if you want to be loved by anyone else. When possible, apologize to the people that you have hurt. By doing so, you humble yourself and acknowledge your mistakes. It also gives them the opportunity to forgive. Forgiveness is powerful. It sets people free from hurt, anger, resentment, and bitterness. It allows joy to come back into your life.

If you ever think that there is no hope, and suicide is the answer, think again. That is a permanent solution to a temporary problem. Life is hard. Loss is hard. But suicide is *never* the answer. If you are ever that close to giving up, please reach out to someone. We are not better off without you if you choose that route. You leave people grieving sometimes for the rest of their lives, especially if you have children. Please don't do that to them. Remember that as long as you are alive, there is hope. You end all hope when you take your own life. Suicide is a demonic spirit—another lie of the enemy. Don't let him win.

We often have false beliefs about ourselves. Those beliefs can be from our own negative thinking. It could be from words spoken over us during our lives. It could have been from a parent. It can be straight from the enemy as he tries to beat us down and keep us from our true identity. We end up agreeing with those false beliefs and accept that we aren't good enough. Maybe we think that we'll never measure up. That's why it's important to go to the word of God, the Bible. In there you will find the truth about yourself. The Word is our measuring stick. We aren't who society says we are. We are who God says we are.

You are important to God. If you weren't, you wouldn't be here. God knitted you together in your mother's womb. He knew you from the foundation of the earth. You are fearfully and wonderfully made. He knows every hair on your head. He has called you for a purpose. You may not have found your purpose, but you have purpose. He created you on purpose. Find out what that purpose is, and you'll find supernatural peace and joy that can't be found in a pill, a person, a place, or any "thing."

CHAPTER 11

Don't Give Up on Others

Then Jesus told his disciples a parable to show them that they should always pray and not give up. He said: "In a certain town there was a judge who neither feared God nor cared what people thought. And there was a widow in that town who kept coming to him with the plea, 'Grant me justice against my adversary.' "For some time he refused. But finally he said to himself, 'Even though I don't fear God or care what people think, yet because this widow keeps bothering me, I will see that she gets justice, so that she won't eventually come and attack me!' And the Lord said, "Listen to what the unjust judge says. And will not God bring about justice for his chosen ones, who cry out to him day and night? Will he keep putting them off? I tell you, he will see that they get justice, and quickly. However, when the Son of Man comes, will he find faith on the earth?"

—Luke 18:1–8 NIV

Without faith, it is impossible to please God. He isn't moved by need. We often think, "God you know my need!" Or, we say, "God knows the need." But God isn't moved by need. He is moved by faith. It's our faith that moves the hand of God. Our whole Christian experience is based on faith, and the way that we exercise our faith in God is through prayer.

"Prayer is the earthly license for heavenly interference," according to Dr. Myles Munroe. In his book *Understanding the Purpose and Power of Prayer*, he says, "Prayer is calling forth what God has already purposed and predestined." It's calling down that which is already in heaven—healing, deliverance, restoration. It's always God's will that we walk in freedom. Jesus died for our sickness and disease as well as for our sins, so we know that it is God's will that we are delivered. It's His will too that your sons and daughters are delivered.

Mark Batterson tells us in his book *Draw the Circle* to pray long prayers. Not hour long prayers, although sometimes that's necessary. But pray until you see the answer just like the persistent widow did. You may have to pray for a long, long time. Don't give up praying because you don't see the changes that you are asking for. Trust that God is working behind the scenes. Somebody has got to stand in the gap, meaning the gap between that person and God. It might as well be you that stands in that position. We've got to fight for and believe for restoration for our loved ones. And oftentimes, the fighting position is on our knees. In his book *All In*, Mark says, "It's time to quit living as if the purpose of life is to arrive safely at death." That's a bold statement. It gets us off the couch and onto our knees.

"For our struggle is not against flesh and blood, but against the rulers, against the authorities, against the powers of this dark world and against the spiritual forces of evil in the heavenly realms." What Paul is saying here in Ephesians 6:12 is that your real enemy is not your loved one. It really isn't a person at all. Spiritual forces are waging war in the spirit realm, and it affects us here on the Earth. The devil—Satan—is after you and your loved ones. This gets deep, but he hates us. Why? Because mankind is made in the image of God, and he hates God. There really is a fight against good and evil. So you do have an enemy, but your enemy isn't a person. You and your loved one are on the same team against the enemy of your souls. He has come to kill, to steal, and to destroy.

Remember the story in the book of Daniel where the Lord told Daniel that He heard him when he prayed the first time. Daniel 10:12–13 says, "Do not be afraid, Daniel. Since the first day that you set your mind to gain understanding and to humble yourself before your God, your words were heard, and I have come in response to them. But the prince of the Persian kingdom resisted me twenty-one days. Then Michael, one of the chief princes, came to help me, because I was detained there with the king of Persia." God hears you when you pray. Sometimes, the answer is delayed. But God is faithful. For that you can be certain!

Bethel Music has a powerful song called "Take Courage." The words are:

> Take courage my heart.
> Stay steadfast my soul.
> He's in the waiting.
> He's in the waiting.

So, there are times that we have to wait. None of us like to wait, but God isn't limited by time. He's never in a hurry. That's an earthly mind-set. Oftentimes, things get worse before they get better. When we don't get the answer or see the person change like we'd like for them to, remember that God heard your prayer. He's working behind the scenes. There are times that God is strategically placing people in the path of your loved one. Sometimes, He's allowing them to go through some really difficult things. He doesn't make those things happen but He allows certain things to happen to help prepare us for our future. It may be that they're working on their testimony. They don't know that at the time. My testimony wouldn't be what it is had God not allowed those things to happen to me. He allowed me to get to a place where I was ready for change. You can't tell someone else when they've had enough. That's entirely up to them.

Remember that God is with you. He will strengthen you and help you to get through what you're going through. He will never leave you or forsake you, according to scripture. Pray long prayers. Hang in there. Keep the faith. Don't give up. These things may sound cliché, but it's crucial for deliverance, healing, or salvation for our loved ones. Remember, God is aware of the situation, and nothing is too big for God.

CHAPTER 12

Don't Give Up on God

Now to Him who is able to do immeasurably more than all
we ask or imagine, according to His power that is at work
within us, to Him be glory in the church and in Christ Jesus
throughout all generations, for ever and ever! Amen.

—Ephesians 3:20–21 NIV

Sometimes people make the mistake of blaming God when things go wrong. God doesn't cause things to go bad. We live in a fallen world. God is there to help us pick up the pieces and move forward once those things happen. Don't be mad at the greatest source of help that there is. Sometimes, all we can say is, "God, I don't understand this, but I trust you." We cannot understand everything that happens or that God allows. We do know that God sees the big picture, and His plans for us are good. He can take those things that the enemy meant for harm, and He can turn it to good. God is faithful! He has not and never will give up on you.

In Bob Beaudine's book *2 Chairs*, he asks "three simple but disruptive questions." Does God know your situation? Is it too hard for Him to handle? Does He have a good plan for you? If you know God at all, you know the answers to these questions. You know that God knows your situation. God is all-knowing. Is it too hard for Him to handle? Nothing is too big for God. Does He have a good plan for you? Always! Then know that "all things work together for good to them that love God, to them who are the called according to his purpose" (Romans 8:28 KJV).

There are times that we have to turn up the volume on our prayers, but I'm not saying pray louder. Sometimes we have to not only pray but fast along with our prayers. We have to include something physical (fasting) to go along with the spiritual (prayer). Jentzen Franklin teaches a lot on fasting. I've heard him say, "Physical obedience brings spiritual release." The King James Version of Matthew 17:21 says, "Howbeit this kind goeth not out but by prayer and fasting."

Also, the word tells us that if any two on earth agree, it shall be done. There is a lot of instruction for praying in the book of Matthew.

> Truly I tell you, whatever you bind on earth will be bound in heaven, and whatever you loose on earth will be loosed in heaven. Again, truly I tell you that if two of you on earth agree about anything they ask for, it will be done for them by my Father in heaven. For where two or three gather in my name, there am I with them. (Matthew 18:18–20 NIV)

What if not giving up on God isn't about God at all? What if it means that we follow God even if He doesn't answer our prayer in the way that we were hoping for? Has He not done enough already that we can say, "Lord, if you never do another thing for me, I owe you my life"? Did He save your soul? Did He change your life? What about "yet not my will, but yours be done"? Those were the words of Jesus as He prayed on the Mount of Olives as recorded in Luke 22:42—total and complete surrender to the will of the Father.

I think that the real disruptive questions that we should ask are about what we're willing to do rather than what God is going to do. Will we never leave or forsake Him? Are we fans, or are we followers of Jesus? Will we follow Him no matter what? Jesus was willing to go to the cross for our sakes. Are we willing to lay it all down for Him?

PART 5

Serving Jesus Christ

CHAPTER 13

The Power of Your Testimony

And they overcame him by the blood of the Lamb, and by the word
of their testimony; and they loved not their lives unto the death.

—Revelation 12:11 KJV

There's something powerful about your testimony. It is how you came
to know the Lord. You are an eyewitness to your experience. It isn't
hearsay. It isn't secondhand knowledge. It is your own account of how
your life was changed when you accepted Christ as your personal savior.

Some testimonies are dramatic. Others are not so messy. To me,
the most powerful testimony is when a person never has to hit bottom
before he or she recognizes the need for a personal relationship with
Christ. Either way, we all have to come to a place in our lives where we
don't just know about God. We have to know God personally. We have
to have that personal relationship with the Lord Jesus Christ because
that is the only way we're going to be content in this life, and it's the
only way that we will be prepared for the life to come. It will not be by
our works or because we grew up in church. It won't be because our

parents were Christians. It won't even be because we behaved well. It will be because we recognized that apart from Christ, we are lost.

Our testimony is as unique as our fingerprint. A person can argue with what you believe but he or she cannot argue with your experience. No one can say we overcame our sin on our own. We know what we experienced. We know that there has been a change in our lives and that we are more content than we ever were before. We know that no drug, or person, or thing has ever satisfied the emptiness in our souls like the Lord has been able to satisfy.

Sharing my testimony isn't easy. I lived to tell some things that the enemy never intended me to tell. He has made it hard for me to share my story. He has tried to make it dark and ugly—a secret that I should keep to myself.

My husband and I went to Haiti on a mission trip in August of 2014 with some members of our church. While we were in one of the villages, visiting the residents, we met a woman. I asked her when she had come to know the Lord, and she told us at age twenty-three. I told her, through a translator, that I too had come to know the Lord around that same age. I began to tell her briefly about what the Lord had done for me at that time—how He had delivered me from drug abuse and rewrote my life story. She began to cry and told us that she had three children that she had to give up because she was unable to take care of them. We prayed for her and spoke words of encouragement before going about our walk through the village. That evening when we returned to the Mission of Hope campgrounds, I told some of the group more of my story.

I was not prepared for the spiritual attack that I experienced as we finished out our day. The enemy, Satan, came at me with both barrels. I don't remember a time that I was so bombarded with words to silence me. Things such as:

You did it again; you told that story!

How could you? These people can't even relate to that!

You've embarrassed our pastor!

You've made this trip about you!

You should never tell that story again!

I have to admit that I was beginning to cower down until he said that last sentence. How could I say that I'd never tell that story again? I can't possibly make that promise. God did something powerful in my life, and I had no right to keep it to myself. However, I couldn't ignore the words of the enemy. I stayed silent again for another two years. The enemy has tried to turn my victorious transformation into a dark secret that he wanted me to hide and to never tell. But God says that I overcome the enemy by the blood of the lamb and the word of my testimony!

That's why Satan wants us to stay quiet. Because we will overcome all of the past mistakes, all of the past fears, and all of the past setbacks when we apply the blood of Jesus to our lives and remember what He has done for us. And when we share that truth with others, hope springs into their lives as well.

Can you imagine feeling hopeless about your life or your child's life, but you hear what God did for someone else and how He changed that person's life? Suddenly, your faith arises, and you believe!

I'm currently counseling female inmates at the city jail where I live. Their difficult stories come home with me. Some, I knew their parents back in the day, and I know the things that they were exposed to and how they were raised. I understand their behavior. But God is the same yesterday, today, and forever. He is no respecter of persons. What He did for me, He'll do for them.

One young lady that heard me speak during one of the chapel services said that she knew if God did that for me, then she knew that there was hope for her. Yes, there is hope for her! God is a life-changer! He is a way-maker when we put our hope and our trust in Him.

Share your story. Tell others what God did for you. Encourage them to put their hope in Jesus.

CHAPTER 14

Sharing Your Faith

Then Jesus came to them and said, "All authority in heaven
and on earth has been given to me. Therefore go and make
disciples of all nations, baptizing them in the name of the
Father and of the Son and of the Holy Spirit, and teaching
them to obey everything I have commanded you. And
surely I am with you always, to the very end of the age."

—Matthew 28:18–20 NIV

It seems to me that when you have had a real salvation experience and
you fully grasp the reality of eternity, it would impossible not to share
with others their need for Christ. I cannot bear the thought of anyone
going into hell for all of eternity. I feel that I have been given and have
received an assignment from the Lord to do my best to see that all of my
family members are saved. For years now, I have prayed, "Lord, please
don't let any of my family go into eternity without you!"

When your family sees the transformation in your life, it can be
bothersome to some yet encouraging to others. I've heard it said that a

person went "from one extreme to another" as if that's a bad thing. If something real has happened in a person's life, you should see change.

A couple of years after my own conversion, I prayed the prayer of salvation with my Uncle Bobby when he was in the hospital. A year or two later, I prayed with my brother, Wayland, as he was dying of cancer. After that, I prayed with my mom before she passed away due to congestive heart failure.

Just after my mom's funeral service, I asked some friends to pray with me about my dad. I wanted to ask God to touch my dad in some way while his heart was still tender due to the loss of my mom. Two days after her funeral, I was at his house eating my lunch when the Lord said, "Now." I said, "But, God, I'm eating." I heard again in my spirit: "Now." "But what if …?" "Now," He said. So I put my sandwich down and said, "Daddy, when are you gonna pray that prayer that Mama prayed?" He answered, "I don't know if I can get through it." I responded with, "I'll help you." I moved next to where he was seated in his favorite chair. I said, "Daddy, do you believe that Jesus is the son of God and that He died on the cross for our sins?" He tilted his head and said, in his most studious way, "As best as I can understand it." I said, "Daddy, the good news is that you don't have to understand it. You just have to accept it."

Right there, I prayed the prayer of salvation, and my daddy repeated it after me. It was the first time that I had ever heard my daddy pray. He was seventy-nine.

Not long after that, my Uncle Bill had a stroke and was in the hospital. I went and prayed with him, and he passed away just a few days later. I had a chance to minister to my cousin, Jerry Don, when I found out that he had cancer.

After attending Jerry's funeral in Valliant, Oklahoma, Charlie and I went to the lake and saw our neighbor who was nearing his final days. It was his last time to visit his lake house. I felt the Lord tug at my heart to ask him about his relationship with Christ, but I refused because I felt my calling was to my family. Rather than being obedient to the still, small voice of the Lord, I reasoned my way out of having that conversation. I may have been the last Christian that he encountered before his passing. Although I don't know what his spiritual condition was, I have vowed to never do that again because my decision still haunts me.

You will be a witness to others whether you talk to them or not. Sometimes, you will be the only Jesus that people will ever see. Your life is a testimony of what Christ can do, so it's important to represent him well. It's important to be a credible witness. You aren't expected to be perfect, but just know that people are watching. Life won't be without problems, but if you'll keep your trust in Christ, they'll watch, and they will want what you have.

A few years ago, Charlie, my daughter Mardi, and I were watching a movie at home on a Sunday night. My brother-in-law's sister called me from Houston, concerned about his spiritual condition. Jimmy had just been diagnosed with pancreatic cancer and wasn't expected to live long. She wanted me to talk to him. I promised her that I would, and we went back to our movie after hanging up the phone. However, there was no way that I could sit there knowing that my brother-in-law could pass away at any time, and we weren't sure where he would spend eternity. I left the others to the movie and went to see him.

When I got to his house, I explained to him that his sister had called me and was concerned about his spiritual condition. We talked, and he told me that he believed that Jesus was the son of God and that He died for our sins. We prayed the prayer of salvation that night. A few days later, he was seen waving to someone that we could not see. Later that day, he took his last breath on earth and went into eternity. We believe he was waving to someone that he knew on the other side, and he joined that person that evening. It doesn't get any better than that!

When the moment presents itself, and it will, ask people if they know Christ as their personal savior. It will be the most important question they will ever be asked. If the Holy Spirit is drawing them, you could be the person to lead them in that important prayer of repentance. It may be that you are sowing a seed that someone else will come along and harvest. Whoever reaps the harvest really isn't important. What is important is our obedience. Do what you are asked to do and leave the rest up to God.

We can't take any material thing from this earth to heaven with us when we go, but we can take people. That will be our greatest reward. I believe that we will hear those coveted words: "Well done, thou good and faithful servant: thou hast been faithful over a few things, I will make thee ruler over many things: enter thou into the joy of thy lord" (Matthew 25:23).

CHAPTER 15

Prayer of Salvation

In the same way, I tell you, there is rejoicing in the presence
of the angels of God over one sinner who repents.

—Luke 15:10 NIV

The most important decision that you will ever make in your lifetime is
to accept Christ as your personal savior. It will change your life eternally.
Romans 10:9–10 says, "If you declare with your mouth, 'Jesus is Lord,'
and believe in your heart that God raised him from the dead, you will
be saved. For it is with your heart that you believe and are justified, and
it is with your mouth that you profess your faith and are saved."

If you believe that Jesus died on the cross as payment for your sins,
that you accept that as truth and want to receive Him as your savior,
pray the following prayer:

Dear Jesus,

I believe that you are the son of God and that you died on a cross
for my sins. I believe that you rose again three days later. I confess my
sin before you and ask for your forgiveness. I ask that you come into

my heart. I receive you as my Lord and Savior. Thank you for loving me. Thank you for forgiving me. Thank you for saving me. It's in your name that I pray.

Amen.

If you prayed that prayer and are sincere in praying it, you are born again. You are now a child of God! You are forgiven, and you are saved! God made salvation simple. He didn't try to complicate it. Accepting Christ is easy but walking it out will be more challenging. You will make mistakes along the way because we aren't perfect, and we never will be on this side of heaven.

That's why it's important to get a Bible and read it. It's also important to surround yourselves with other people that are on the same journey. That's where the church comes in. The people there will not be perfect. You might get hurt. You might get offended, but don't let Satan rob you of what God wants to do in your life! Get into a Bible-believing church and watch your life begin to be transformed! It's worth the effort that it takes to get there!

CONCLUSION

I press on toward the goal to win the prize for which
God has called me heavenward in Christ Jesus.

—Philippians 3:14 NIV

Life is a series of starts and stops, embracing and letting go, hellos and
goodbyes. It's not always people or relationships or places. It's thinking,
feeling, believing, and pursuing. It's habits and behaviors. It's faith. It's
trust. It's hope. It's remembering and forgetting. It's pushing aside and
then recalling.

It's learning to love ourselves as we are, trusting that we are fearfully
and wonderfully made, knitted together in our mother's womb. It's
growing older and wiser, accepting each stage of our lives. It's reaching
out to others with encouraging words reminding them that there's
always hope and to never give up.

I have found it helpful to accept that I don't have to be completely
satisfied with life on this Earth 100 percent of the time. Rather than
questioning myself why I'm not just overflowing with joy every day, I
recognize that we are not of this world. There's a longing for our eternal
home whether we understand it or not, Christian or non-Christian. We
all have that void that only Christ can fill. We are spirit beings having
a human experience, and the human experience is temporary.

Recently, I was invited to take the position as senior chaplain over
the jail ministry where I have been volunteering for the past two years.
As I prayerfully considered the opportunity, I realized that people have

more regrets for the things not done in their lives than regretting the things that they do. So I decided to step out in faith and accept the offer.

On the first day of my new job, God confirmed that I was right where I was supposed to be. I learned on that day that the current chief of police, who offered me the job as chaplain, was the officer who first responded to my call when I had been shot with the arrow thirty-six years ago. I'm telling you, you cannot make this stuff up. God continues to light my path and confirm my steps as I make myself available to Him. I'm so thankful for His faithfulness!

Being vulnerable and sharing my story by writing this book has not been easy for me. There are things that to this day, in speaking of those dark days that I lived through, I'm not certain were real or not. The circumstances of those days leave some things unclear.

What I do know, however, is that God saved me for a reason, and He's not finished with me yet. God saw fit to extend His hand that I could grab a hold of, and He pulled me to safety. It's not time for me to go sit on the sidelines. It's not time to quit attending church. It's not time to stop leading or attending small groups. It's not time to quit living for God and sharing my faith. God has more for me to do.

As I was wrapping up this conclusion, a friend shared this scripture, and I think it's worth including. In 1 Corinthians 9:22–23 Paul writes, "To the weak I became weak, to win the weak. I have become all things to all people so that by all possible means I might save some. I do all this for the sake of the gospel that I may share in its blessings." I looked back in my Bible, and on June 20, 2018, I had written above that same passage, "Whatever it takes."

I have prayed for those that God would have read this book. I asked that He would use it to encourage, challenge, and push people out of their comfort zones. I asked Him to help parents recommit to praying fervently for their lost children and believe that they will be saved. I pray that people will invite others to know Christ by sharing their faith and their testimonies. It is my prayer that men or women bound by drugs will believe that what God did for me, He will do for them because His word says in Acts 10:34, "God does not show favoritism." He is not a respecter of persons.

Position yourself to receive your miracle by allowing your faith to be increased. Our God is faithful!

Charlie's 50th Birthday Celebration

Susan and Charlie 30th Anniversary

Susan and Charlie
Christmas 2016

Susan and Charlie on a Cruise
and Susan - Jamaica

Susan's Family. Dad, Mom, Siblings

Wedding Day

ABOUT THE AUTHOR

Susan Roberts has lived in Midwest City, OK all of her life. She has worked in the medical field for more than twenty-five years in administrative roles. Retired from her full time job, she has recently accepted the position of Senior Chaplain for the inmates at the Midwest City Jail.

Susan is passionate about leading people to Christ. She shares her faith with those that are in jail and encourages them to pursue a vision for their lives greater than what they are living. She also prays regularly that not one of her family members will go into eternity without God and has had the privilege of leading many of them to Christ.

Susan married her husband, Charlie, in 1985 and they have three adult daughters. She and Charlie are committed to regular church attendance and serve in various ministries at their home church in Midwest City.

Printed in the United States
By Bookmasters